the other shepards

Also by Adele Griffin

Rainy Season
Split Just Right
Sons of Liberty

the other shepards

Adele Griffin

hyperion books for children

new york

For Jody

Many thanks to my editor, Donna Bray,
for all her support and encouragement.

Copyright © 1998 by Adele Griffin.

FIRST EDITION

3 5 7 9 10 8 6 4

This book is set in 11-point Palatino.

Library of Congress Cataloging-in-Publication Data:
Griffin, Adele
The Other Shepards / Adele Griffin
p. cm.
Summary: Teenage Holland and her younger sister Geneva, having
always lived under the shadow of siblings who died before they were
born, struggle to establish separate identities and escape from the
oppressive weight of their parents continuing grief.
ISBN: 0-7868-0423-8 (trade : alk. paper)
ISBN 0-7868-2370-4 (lib. : alk paper)
[1. Sisters—Fiction. 2. Identity—Fiction. 3. Family problems—Fiction.
4. Grief—Fiction. 5. New York (N.Y.)—Fiction.]
I. Title. PZ7.G8813250t 1998
[Fic]—dc21 98-12609

contents

geneva

"She okay?"

"Oh, yes, fine. She's fine."

"Don't look so good. Your sister?"

"Yes. She's fine. It's elevators. She hates them."

Geneva hears us but her eyes don't move from lighted button number nine, its glowing promise of escape.

"Hard thing to hate, living in Manhattan." The man's smile rests on Geneva, who stretches her mouth into a straight line. I smile back at him instead, as I squeeze the tips of my sister's sweating fingers.

The elevator pings to a stop on the fourth floor. The man gets off and a largish woman steps on, candy-coated in perfume and eating into our space with her sturdy backside and pocketbook.

"Five more floors and we're done," I say. Geneva blinks. A dew of sweat breaks at the hairline above her pulsing temple.

"My neck is closing in on me," she whispers. "I can't breathe. I need to find a bathroom." The woman cuts her eyes at Geneva. I know my sister feels the stare by the way she scowls and shrivels into her coat.

"Is that White Rain?" I say to distract the woman, although I know it's not White Rain because that's Mom's scent.

Her eyes soften. "Rose water," she answers, touching two fingers to her collarbone. "It's just rose water, dear. I've worn it since I was young."

I nod. "It's really nice."

"You could get some for yourself at Bigelow's."

Using just enough voice for me to hear, Geneva whispers, "Thumbkin." Then she begins mouthing the Hail Mary at hyperspeed. I frown hard to close up my smile, now that it strikes me how the woman does resemble Thumbkin, a stern, pointy-faced elf from one of our old bedtime stories. Geneva has a terrible knack for fitting the perfect word onto a person, neat as a hat to a head.

"Is she all right?" The woman tilts her Thumbkin chin toward Geneva.

"Oh, she'll be fine. Elevators make her tense."

I look over at Geneva, who is racing through her words—"Artthouamongwomenblessedisthefruit"—and my mind thumbs through bathroom possibilities. Carr's probably won't have one for customers, but there's one in the lobby, except you have to get the key from the grumpy doorman, who I didn't see on the way up. But isn't there a Chinese restaurant right across the street and down half a block? I have to be sure. I don't know much about this Flatiron district building, except that it's mostly gallery space and some specialty shops, and I can't just spin Geneva up and around these breathless heights and spaces. I pounce to a decision.

"We'll get Mrs. Motahahn to help us."

As the elevator opens, Geneva flings herself free, galloping to the end of the hallway, where she heaves open the glass door inscribed with a whispery frost of cursive announcing CARR'S ARTISTIC EXPRESSIONS. I follow more sedately, betting myself: *if you can walk only on the diagonal patterns of the wood without stepping out of line, then Geneva gets a bathroom.*

Mrs. Motahan's eyes entreat me as soon as I've opened the door. Geneva's head turtles into her shoulders. "I'm sorry, Geneva, but you'll have to use the one in the lobby. You should have thought . . ."

"We better go now, Holland," she says. "I need to go."

"Oh, please, Mrs. Motahahn, she's very sick!" My voice unhinges to a squeak. Customers' heads stiffen, listening. "She really needs that bathroom. It's the flu. She's been sick all week. My parents didn't want me to take her out today, so this is all completely my fault. I'm such a dummy, dragging her uptown."

"But . . . I don't think, and with Mrs. Carr not here right now . . ." Mrs. Motahahn draws her pen from her cap of silver hair and taps an uncertain beat against her palm.

"Please. It's all my fault. I don't think there's time to take her downstairs."

"I mean, it's just for, it's not really for, but if she might be sick, we do have, ah, have, um . . ." Mrs. Motahahn scrutinizes Geneva, then shakes her head. "Wait here, girls."

"She's getting the key," I say under my breath as we watch Mrs. Motahahn wriggle out from behind the counter and disappear behind a back door. "Another few seconds and you'll have a room all to yourself. Then you can do whatever, run water, whatever."

Geneva's bathroom emergencies depend on her illness. Sometimes she needs the toilet, or at least needs to be near it; other times she has to wash her hands and face until she feels calm and sanitized. She usually performs her water rituals alone, although I have stood by her in more than a few public rest rooms, glaring off onlookers as my sister repeatedly splats a cupped hand with the pink or lemon-yellow liquid soap, then rinses herself into a sense of calm. Not even the professional help our parents have employed over the years can make sense of Geneva's problem; her explanation that water "fixes me" is all we have to go by.

I rest my hand lightly on her arm, over the rough boiled wool of her car coat. I wear the same style coat, the same color gray. We wear berets to match, and beneath our coats, identical gray and yellow plaid kilts: the colors of Monsignor Ambrose, our school on West Thirteenth Street. The only difference is that I wear a yellow sweater, to show that I am in eighth grade, while Geneva is outfitted in the (uglier) gray vest of a sixth grader.

"What if she won't let me? What'll I do, Holland? If she says no? If I'm sick all over the floor?" Geneva's voice is a sprinkling of sound. I once read that blue whales communicate with their kin by sending out low-frequency sound waves that extend for thousands of miles. Sometimes I believe that this is the way I must hear Geneva's voice: sneaky tremors reverberating under my feet, shinnying up my spinal cord to my brain.

"Stop, you'll only work yourself into feeling sicker. We'll get the key. Here comes Mrs. Motahahn now. She's waving for you to follow her. Go ahead, it's okay." I steer my sister behind the counter to where Mrs. Motahahn beckons. Geneva hesitates, then darts off.

Alone, I can relax into being a regular customer. I trail up and down the aisles, peering into glass-fronted cases. It was my idea to cab up to Carr's after school to find Mom's birthday present, but I didn't tell Geneva about my plan until lunchtime, which probably wasn't enough warning. Although I would have been happier to come by myself and let Geneva take half credit for the gift, she insisted on joining me. She always insists.

"I'll be good," she promised from her solitary perch on the windowsill of the gym, her favorite position during indoor recess. "I'll help."

"Are you sure?" She was chewing her lip, and I knew that she was not sure, only stubborn, but it would bruise her to think I'd rather go shopping on my own.

Now I wish I hadn't told her.

"You said flu?" Mrs. Motahahn squints worriedly at me from behind the counter. "Holland? A flu?"

"Oh, yes. She's been terrible all week."

"Poor girl, it's going around. You keep drinking that orange juice, or your parents'll have their hands full. So there's a little bud vase we just got in, third shelf from the bottom, right side, Holland, right side, Art Deco but not too arty, soft-paste porcelain, very sweet. Reminds me of your mom. When you phoned earlier, it kept running through my head all afternoon what would be right." Mrs. Motahahn lowers her voice. "And it's reasonable, cost-wise."

The vase is pretty, a celery-green teardrop, and a quick flip-over confirms that Mrs. Motahahn is right about the price, too.

"This is perfect, Mrs. Motahahn. She'll love it. Can we get it gift-wrapped? I'll pay the extra." I pretend to scratch my knee and stealthily remove the chunky billfold wedged in my sock. Money is something I'm more comfortable saving than spending, and as soon as so much as a dollar leaves my music box bank, I need to feel it pressed up against my skin until it's time for us to part.

"Oh, aren't you a sweet thing. Gift wrap's complimentary. Not like at the big stores." Mrs. Motahahn takes the vase from my hands and begins stuffing its insides with tissue paper. "How's Macy's treating your mom these days? It seems like eons ago I left."

"She's in bedding now," I say. "She switched out of housewares last year. She likes it, though. She says it's a nice change of pace."

"Well, I don't envy your job, honey, having to figure out a present for a mother who works in the world's largest department store."

"She'll be glad we came here, to catch up with you. She always says how she wishes you were still at Macy's." Mrs. Motahahn smiles, and I can tell that she's forgotten about Geneva, but I haven't. What will I do if she decides to stay in that bathroom all afternoon? She did that once before, last summer, at an Olive Garden restaurant in New Jersey.

I help Mrs. Motahahn choose a silk ribbon and a tiny gilt-edged card. I ask about Percy, Mrs. Motahahn's Siamese, and she tells me a funny story about how Percy chewed a hole in her favorite wool sweater. I am almost finished signing "love, Holland and Geneva" on the card when my sister emerges from the bathroom, and the "va" of her name is a flourish of relief.

"All done," I say, trying to be brisk but sounding irritated, which I am. Why does Geneva even bother trying if she knows she's never any help? Her drama only makes life difficult for everyone, excluding herself, of course.

"Elevator again," she dares to whine.

"Oh, come on. You're always better at down. Say good-bye to Mrs. Motahahn."

My sister gives a limp wave and watery wedge of smile. I yank her through the doors and down the hall.

"Think of an elevator being like a cool ride in a spaceship," I say, knowing exactly how the horror of this idea will ricochet through Geneva's phobic little brain. Sometimes my patience gets eaten up by meaner urges, but it doesn't seem fair that I always have to be the older, responsible one. For just one day, I'd like to see Geneva try being the big sister while I make the embarrassing scenes.

"Brett and Carla are coming for cake tonight," Mom told me at breakfast this morning. "And they're bringing the baby. Please try not to be an Ick." *Ick* is Mom's special word to describe anything that is overly touchy or sentimental.

Mom does not realize that my Ickness is inborn. Whether I am trailing my fingers across the surface of freshly folded bed sheets, savoring a mocha-chip ice-cream cone, or dabbing on some of my favorite perfume (Woods of Windsor's Lily-of-the-Valley), my senses of touch and taste and smell are overwhelming delights. Mom prefers air kisses and thank-you notes: a look-but-don't-touch kind of politeness.

"Freddie?" My mouth and fingertips were prickling, already itching to kiss and rub baby Freddie's head, soft and warm and bald as a dinner roll. "Do you think they'll let me hold him or change him or feed him or anything?"

Over her tea mug, Mom's eyebrows shifted like wary antennae. "All I ask is that you don't make people feel uncomfortable."

Geneva is the opposite of Ick. She inches through her day inside an invisible plastic bubble. She shrugs off the hugs of overfriendly relatives and teachers. She hates participating in sports because they force you to smell other people's sweat. She even flinches at television kisses. When people say Geneva and I are alike, what they mean is that we are close, the way spring and summer melt together but are separate and distinct.

On the drive down from Carr's, Geneva sits up straight in the cab, her hands stapled together in her lap, her spine a tilted axis from the green-black plastic seat back, her face uplifted, her eyes closed. I know she is worn out from her earlier dramatics, upset that she didn't have a say on Mom's gift, and probably faintly nauseous from thinking about cab germs. I feel sorry for her, and I relent.

"Mom will like how we bought her present from Mrs. Motahahn, especially since Carr's salespeople work on commission," I volunteer. "And did you know Brett and Carla are bringing baby Freddie tonight?"

There is no visible reaction from her brittle body. "I bet he has some teeth by now," I say after a few more blocks.

Silence.

We turn off Fifth Avenue on Ninth Street, nosing west through the crosstown traffic. Tight green buds are beginning to appear on the dogwood trees. Soon they will unpack into friendly white blossoms, softly loosening along with the pink, tongue-shaped blooms of our window box bleeding hearts. Spring in the Village. Nowhere else in the city looks or smells more luscious.

"I hate it when Brett comes," Geneva says abruptly. "It'll be weird. The parents get strange."

"I like Brett."

"I like *him*, I hate the *visit*." Geneva turns and her eyes are like a pair of tacks, pushing into me. "Last time he was here he told me I looked like Kevin. Spitting image, he said."

"What? No, you don't. You look like me and I look like you. Everyone says so. Medium sized, reddish brownish hair, blue eyes, kind of freckly. That's us."

"Dad once said I looked like Kevin, too," Geneva muses.

"Kevin? Ha, Kevin was short and round and had pink skin. Pink as a shrimp. I bet he always got sunburned."

"Watch out how you talk, Holland," Geneva warns. "Kevin can hear every word. His feelings might be hurt."

"He *was* pink. It's no insult."

Geneva slides her gaze to the ceiling of the cab and mutters something.

"You better not be apologizing to Kevin for me. Are you?"

"Mom always tells us how angels can hear everything. Plus, the Bible says they answer straight to God. If you do or say something bad, the angels have to report you."

"Geneva," I say, exasperated, "heaven isn't like the principal's office."

"I didn't know you were such an expert," she retorts airily. "By the way, don't tell Mom or Dad about Carr's. Mom thinks I'm getting better. Don't tell."

"I wouldn't. Why would I? And I think you are getting better."

Geneva shakes her head. "Nobody else acts like me. Nobody's scared like me."

"You're being very dramatic." I nudge a leg closer to knock it against hers. "Let's get out here and walk to the flower shop. Then we can get a couple tulips for our vase. You pick the color."

The three-story brick townhouse on 176 Waverly Place in Greenwich Village has been my home ever since I was born, only a few blocks away, at St. Vincent's Hospital, and my parents' home for twenty years before that. They bought the entire house during a time when the Village was cheap, since anybody with a regular paying job preferred to live higher than the Forties.

The parents were young and poor, perfect downtown candidates. They met at a bookstore on Bank Street, closed now, that specialized in detective and crime novels. Dad always begins the story of when he first saw Mom by saying, "It was a dark and stormy night," but then confesses that it was actually a cool summer morning and that Mom was working behind the register.

Although they are often praised for their good investment in buying the house, the Village itself does not suit either of them, since they both work in midtown: Mom as a buyer for Macy's and Dad as a research scientist for Biotech Labs, which is an off-campus part of New York University. And whenever they go out, which is rare, it is usually to see a play or a ballet—never to the jazz clubs and poetry corners of our neighborhood. Leaving 176 Waverly, however, is not an option. The house is inlaid and overworked in memories too precious to sell.

Every Saturday morning since I can remember, tour groups have strolled down our street, part of Historic Manhattan, and 176 Waverly's official history has been long overboiled inside my head. "Designed by a student of the popular architect James Renwick, this Victorian Gothic style building—note the leaded-glass fanlight over the door, the wrought-iron stair railing, the open-box newels—was built in 1883. During *prohibition*, Waverly Place was lined with *speakeasies*." (A speakeasy is a place where people could sneak off to buy and drink alcohol during prohibition, which was a law in the 1920s that banned liquor from public and private establishments. After years of hearing the bull-horn-wielding tour guides yak about this, I finally looked up both words.)

The tour always winds up with the story of New York mayor James John Walker's mistress, an actress who lived in our house during the Roaring Twenties. It is rumored that some nights the furtive but well-dressed ghost of "Beau James" can be seen sneaking down the short flight of steps to the sidewalk, where he dissolves into mist as soon as his foot hits the pavement. I have never caught sight of the mayor's ghost, although not for lack of trying. Geneva maintains she's seen him on several occasions, wearing a swirling opera cape and a top hat. She says his eyes are more bashful than you might expect, all things considered.

Waverly is a bent, quiet street, where the most commotion on a given day is the yips of two sparring poodles. In the summer, the poplar and ginkgo trees provide a spangled shade from the sun, although the crushed ginkgo berries under our shoes smell like vomit.

Geneva snuffles at the yellow tulips as she

waits for me to unlock the front door. "They don't smell," she says. "Maybe we should have got roses or lilies."

"Tulips are more cheerful. Besides, you're allergic to roses."

"And don't tell about Carr's."

"You already said. And why would I tell?" I try to bite back the snap in my voice, but I'm tired and distracted, thinking about how I should start digging into my French homework, which tonight means correcting the test I flunked.

"Someone's here," Geneva whispers. I follow my sister's gaze to the dining room window.

"No, no one."

"Someone," she insists. "A lady."

"Ooh, maybe it's the mayor's mistress," I say. "Waiting for one last afternoon of illicit love." But I watch the front windows as I jiggle my keys impatiently at the slide and dead bolt locks. A lady? The parents almost never have visitors. Certainly no one unexpected. I can tell from Geneva's breathing that she's curious, too.

"Hello!" I make my voice brave, like a returning hunter, as we enter the house. "Who's there?"

"No one, just me. Annie. Annie the painter."

It was not fear, exactly, that stirred inside me when I heard her voice, although I have lived in New York City my entire life, and know its many terrible tales of intruders and muggers and worse. I probably should have spun right around and hustled both of us out into the safety of the street. But when my sister tugged at my elbow, stepping past me and walking through the swinging doors into the kitchen, I remember feeling mostly surprise. It was such a strange thing for her to do. And I wondered if Geneva had read my mind, and was trying to be the big sister for a change.

The only thing I could think to do was to follow her.

two
annie

"What was your first impression?" my sister would ask me time and again after we had met Annie, and long after we stopped knowing her. "The first, number one thing that hit you?"

"That she wasn't a redhead," I always answer. I associate the name Annie with the Little Orphan and the one of Green Gables. Both redheads.

This Annie's hair is brilliant blond and wispy, its pollen yellow tint reminding me of the baby picture of Mom that sits on Dad's desk. Her complexion is bright; her forehead, nose, and chin are flushed, as if she has crept too close to a fire, and her pale, smoke-colored eyes regard my sister and me with steady attention.

Geneva remembers thinking that Annie was floating. "She was holding her pencil like a wand, and she was wearing that light blue dress, and the sun was coming in behind her so I had to squint. But when she moved across the kitchen to us, it was like those fairies with the pulleys on their backs from when we saw *A Midsummer Night's Dream* at the Bleecker Street Theater. Or at least," Geneva bites her lip, "that's what I *think* I thought. The kitchen was full of sun. I couldn't see."

Which is strange, because in my mind Annie wears a dark blue dress and the afternoon is overcast. The image is like a negative plate held over Geneva's picture, and looking back, I can't help but mistrust both versions of our memory.

"Annie the painter?" I repeat. "A wall painter or a picture painter?"

"Both. A picture on a wall," Annie says. She reaches a hand to the messy knot of her upswept hair and untwists it. Saffron squiggles fall around her shoulders. "I'm painting the mural for your mom's birthday. Some plants and leaves to look at and cheer her up while she slaves over a hot stove." She points a finger at each of us. "Two Shepard sisters. But which is . . . ?"

"That's Geneva," I say. "I'm Holland."

"Nobody slaves much in this house," says Geneva. "Mostly we defrost."

"Speaking of, who wants a nice warming cup of coffee? My own blend. I'm taking a breather. What do you think of my sketches?" She nods to the kitchen table.

Rolls of vellum paper clutter our table and banquette. The lazy Susan and napkin holder have been pushed aside to accommodate sketch paper and pencils. Several opened books display glossy photographs of landscape paintings and designs. The place mats are stacked on the floor. I suppress an urge to straighten the mess.

"The parents don't like us to drink coffee," Geneva says, creeping toward the table. She bends over a book, her arms wound exaggeratedly behind her back to show she won't touch it. Then she turns and looks at me, her teeth raking her bottom lip, waiting for me to set the situation right. "Do they know she's here?" she whispers.

"You're sure my mom and dad know you're here?" I ask as politely as I can. "I mean, that you're here in our kitchen right now? Because I think they would have told us. It's kind of, whatever, weird, finding a stranger in your own house."

"But it's supposed to be a surprise. From your dad to your mom. Only, when you think about it, the mural is really from me to your mom, since I'm doing all the work. Now why don't you two relax and take off those funny hats. Who wants coffee?"

That's when I notice the powerfully cozy coffee smell wafting through the kitchen. I never drink coffee, but this aroma is like a potion, thick and enticing.

Annie opens a cupboard and pulls out two orange-striped coffee mugs, part of a set of Navajo earthenware we never use anymore. Geneva and I yank off our berets but otherwise remain motionless, watching Annie.

She picks up the pot and pours coffee into mugs. "At least try it. It's a special vanilla nut-meg blend that I invented myself. And I have a bag of cinnamon rolls. There was a day-old sale at My Favorite Muffin. Jack eats there all the time."

"Who's Jack?" I ask.

"Jack's a friend of mine, an actor. In fact, he went out on an audition this morning, a television commercial for heartburn medicine. He

was so funny, talking to himself in the mirror—
'I can't believe all those years of summer stock
for this'—but then he got more positive, which
is just like Jack, telling himself how an actor's
life is not about shortcuts, but persistence
and . . . you want milk?"

We are transfixed, watching Annie bungle
around our kitchen, rummaging for spoons and
milk. She has a dancer's body, long limbs as del-
icately hinged as Japanese brush strokes, but her
movements are fidgety and graceless, as if she
can't figure out how she is centered. I decide the
problem must be her old-fashioned cork-soled
sandals, a style that not only looks uncomfortable but is too summery for the weather.

She jerks to a stop at the kitchen counter and
begins tunneling into a nylon knapsack that is
flopped beside the sink. "In here somewhere, if
you just hold on a minute."

Geneva looks at me and mouths, "Gun." I
shake my head and mouth, "No way." Annie
rummages and mumbles to herself, looking
slightly demented, if not gun-toting.

"Ask," Geneva mouths. I shake my head.

Geneva pulls in a quivering breath and
squeaks, "Who are you? Are you a robber? I
think now is a good time to call Dad or the
authorities to find out—"

With a triumphant "Aha!" Annie whips around, clutching a white paper bag. Geneva screams. It is her usual scream, a spine-scouring pitch that has roused me so many times in the middle of the night that upon hearing it now, I do not even flinch. Annie immediately drops her paper bag and matches Geneva with a scream of her own, although this noise seems more professional and military: a call to arms, a war whoop. Then she claps a hand to her mouth, spreading the fingers of her other hand to touch the pulse points of her neck, and she doubles over laughing. Her laugh is goofy, it sounds like hiccups. I smile. I can't help it.

"I see tomorrow's headline of the *Post*: 'Girls Attacked by Artist Bearing Pastries.'" Annie smiles and bends to retrieve the bag, which she opens and glides beneath Geneva's nose. "Day-old cinnamon rolls. That's all they are. See? Look, it's no joke, I was officially contracted to come to the Shepard residence and create a spectacular mural worthy of your mother's fifty-sixth birthday. I have all the information on me, somewhere." She taps her forehead. "Most important is that it's up here. Anyone will tell you the best plans are stored in the memory."

"Oh, sure," I agree. The smell of coffee dries

my throat and gurgles my stomach, and most of my concentration is focused on tasting it.

"Clear off the table, and then we'll sit down and take a load off. You can tell me which design ideas you like best. How obvious is it that I haven't talked to a single solitary person in a while? I'm going crazy for company. I should have Jack's job. I'd be good at heartburn commercials. 'Oh, Mama, I love your sausage and anchovy pizza, but I sure hate the heartburn.'" Annie makes a sour face and touches her hand to her heart. Then her expression changes to coin-eyed surprise. "'Cohrex? Never heard of it! But hey, I'll try anything to get ridda this pain.'"

I look at Geneva, ready to take my cue from her reaction. Annie's day-old rolls and heartburn monologue might be too much for my sister. A classic Geneva move would be to run upstairs and slam her bedroom door, and I am half-waiting for it. Then I will have to apologize for my sister and spend the next hour coaxing Geneva back into a social mood in time for Mom's birthday dinner. I make a bet. *If Geneva stays, then you have to do all your French conjugations after dinner and not, absolutely not, leave them for last minute tomorrow morning.*

Geneva stands still for a moment, then picks up a mug of coffee, steps lightly to the kitchen table, and roosts on the edge of the banquette. Victorious, I jump to clear off the books.

"There are plates above the stove, Annie, if you want to set the rolls on them. Where should I put your designs? We have half-and-half, too, in the side of the fridge, on the shelf with the jelly and mustard." I'm chatty to hide my surprise. Geneva will stay. No running upstairs, no locked door. What a relief to avoid the usual scene.

The three of us assemble naturally, as if we have always shared coffee and rolls after school. The old, well-grooved routines are blinked out in a moment: Geneva and me arriving home and treading upstairs to our separate bedrooms on the third floor, closing our doors and starting our homework or talking to friends on the telephone. Later, the muffled sounds of the parents home from work and checking the answering machine messages, then opening the mail in the living room.

Annie settles back in her seat and sighs comfortably. "I took a tour earlier, and I saw all the kid portraits in the living room. Geneva is the one holding the doll, right? And you're the one in the picture hat?"

"Yeah, that's us. Mr. Kintsler painted us. He's a famous portrait painter. He even painted some presidents."

"He painted *all* of us," Geneva adds.

I give Geneva a warning look. "Our dad is old school friends with him, so Mr. Kintsler painted a portrait of each of us on our seventh birthdays. The sittings were so long. I remember Dad kept feeding me butterscotch candies so I'd stay still."

"Mmm, once I attempted painting a watercolor of my brothers. Believe me, I'd rather paint pumpkins or trees."

"Well, you could put a lot of trees on our walls for your mural," I suggest. "Even a whole forest, like I saw in one of your books. Our kitchen's pretty big. Don't you think a forest would look cool, Geneva?"

"Three of us are dead."

I knew she would do it. I hoped she wouldn't, but she can never resist the drama. Geneva picks up her coffee and sips it long and slow, lowering her eyes to block out my reaction, letting the rising steam film her face. I could almost slap her. Instead I decide to steal her favorite story and tell it the wrong way. My way. I turn to Annie, who is staring at Geneva and probably trying to figure out what she just heard.

"Our two brothers and our sister died before either of us were born," I begin quickly, and Annie looks away from Geneva to give me her attention. "It's very sad, obviously, except we never knew them. I mean, we wish they were alive, but not the way you would if you had real memories to miss them with."

"It was a terrible accident," Geneva adds, attempting to rekindle the mood that I am working to squelch. "It was all over the newspapers." Geneva usually finds a grim comfort in telling the tale of our family tragedy, as if by spreading the information she can temporarily redistribute its weight. Make it someone else's horror, at least for a little while.

"But it happened a really long time ago, before we were born, like I said," I explain. "Eighteen years ago."

"During Christmas vacation," Geneva adds. "A drunk driver crashed into their jeep. Kevin and John died instantly, but Elizabeth was in a coma for three days."

Annie allows a moment of respectful silence, then she shakes her head sadly and says, "Mmmph."

Over the years that Geneva and I have had to tell this story, we have witnessed hundreds of different reactions. We have seen faces clench into lines of pain, eyes that instantly wet in sympathy or glitter with curiosity or agitation. We have had people, sometimes strangers, buckle over us with crushing hugs and kisses. I usually dislike the reactions almost as much as I hate broadcasting the story, but now, suddenly faced with a stranger's "mmmph," I realize I have come to expect the sympathy, and its absence bothers me.

"It's horrible, we know it's horrible for us," I tell her encouragingly.

"For you?" Annie asks.

"Well, I mean, sure it is. But of course, especially for our mom and dad. Nothing could be worse for parents."

"It's parents' worst nightmare, having their kids die," Geneva adds, a fact beyond dispute, as sure a comment as "it's raining."

Still, Annie is silent. Geneva presses up bits of glazed cinnamon-roll sugar from the table onto her fingertip, then flicks the sugar onto her plate. Under the table, my feet tap impatiently. We are waiting for Annie to agree with us, but the length of her silence bewilders me, and I know Geneva must feel a little surprised, too.

"True. Everyone feels awful for the parents," Annie finally says with a shrug, and in a voice that is empty of emotion. "But it seems to me your mom and dad got a great second chance, right? Another start, blessed with two more kids. Lucky for them."

"I guess, . . . but I don't know," I say. Her words make me twitchy, and I have to hold back an urge to laugh, although I don't know what I find so funny. It is strange to think of the parents as blessed and lucky. People almost never describe them that way.

"The parents had a whole family before us." Geneva's tone is quarrelsome, insistent on a little compassion. "They'll never be truly happy again."

"Don't forget, some people can't have any children. That's as sad a story as any," Annie says in that same voice that contains nothing.

"It's not wrong or selfish for them to miss those other kids." My eyes heat up in defense of the parents and the burden of our family loss. "They probably feel grateful for what they have *and* sad for what was taken from them."

Annie pushes aside her mug and leans toward the pile of sketches heaped on the floor. "I didn't mean to upset you. It's better to concentrate on the living, that's all I meant," she says. "The paintings of those other kids should be stored away if they always start conversations like this. You girls never even knew those kids, and they'll never know you."

"The paintings have a right to be up," I say. "You don't get how it is, to be our family."

"True," Annie answers. "So let's consider this conversation closed."

After the initial shock, most people circle the story of the other Shepards like scuba divers exploring a sunken ship. They creep in slowly with cautious questions but soon become entranced by the tragedy, and so they dart farther and deeper, searching for details. *How did it happen?* A drunk driver was speeding and hit them. *When?* Late at night, Kevin was driving them back in his jeep from a clambake on the beach. *Where were they?* They were on vacation in Saint Germaine, an island in the Caribbean. *Were your parents in the jeep?* No, just one other kid. He survived. How old were they? Kevin was eighteen, John was sixteen, Elizabeth would have been fifteen the following week. *Were they buried over there?* No, the bodies were flown back home. They're all buried together at our church, St. Luke-in-the-Fields. *Is the drunk driver in prison now?* He died in the crash, too.

And so Annie's lack of interest in the accident is baffling. It has to be a first.

"Good," I say to her now, "because Geneva and I don't want to talk about this anymore. It's very personal." Stubborn, stupid words, but closing this conversation should be my job. Even if I sound like a dork.

Annie holds up a sketch. "Let's get back to business. What do you think of this one? Kind of an Impressionist style." Penciled lines curl into tendrils of flowers and wild plants. The sketch is smudged, messy and wild. "Of course, there are other styles: Cretan, Etruscan, I think I have a book of paintings by Uccello around here somewhere. We need to pick an inspiring theme."

"How about someplace beautiful and far away, like Tahiti?" suggests Geneva. My eyes follow her fingers tracing raggedy pictures in the air. "Paint red and orange and yellow flowers. With snapdragons and lilies. And a parrot and . . . like that!" She raps her knuckles over a picture of a bird displayed in one of Annie's books. "Only with more feathers."

"Good, great. Like Gauguin." Annie nods in agreement. "You talk like a real artist."

I listen, surprised, as Geneva lifts off into a story of how she really likes art but not Mr. Tegal's art class at school because he plans too many paper-cut collage projects, and she prefers paints. It's common knowledge that Geneva is the artistic one of the two of us, but I have never heard my sister talk about school, or art, so energetically.

"What's your favorite medium—watercolor, acrylic, or oil?" Annie asks, which throws open the window of another conversation about oils, Andrew Wyeth, and the best way to get turpentine out of your hair. (Annie's recommendation is to shampoo with white vinegar and a tablespoon of salt.) It is so rare, and so enjoyable, to hear Geneva talk to a stranger that I myself keep quiet.

We finish our coffee, and Geneva and I tear the last cinnamon bun in half.

"Oh, my gosh, look at the time!" Annie taps her watch and springs clumsily out of her chair. I am amazed that she hasn't spilled or broken anything yet. "I better go. These sketches are for your dad to give your mom. Sort of as the birthday appetizer before the main dish. She decides what she likes best, and you can report back to me. You'll help me out, right? See you, then."

Annie swirls into her coat, an oversized linen blazer that is too lightweight to be of much use in March, then she grabs her knapsack and is gone, clattering out the kitchen door, the clop of her shoes fading as she walks down the steps and through the alleyway.

"I don't think I've ever seen that window open," I remark as we carry our mugs and dishes to the sink.

"Such a funny lady," Geneva says. "Although I kind of doubt she had an appointment anywhere; her watch was way off. She was just finished being here is all."

"Most painters keep their own schedules," I say. "I wonder how Dad even heard about her? Maybe she's from the art department of the University?"

"Maybe. How old do you think she is?"

"Early thirties, I'd guess. She acts younger, though, like a kid. The way she was so interested in our school, asking us all those questions. Except for she's wrong about Elizabeth and Kevin and John not being our real family. That was mean."

"She didn't say it the way you heard it. You never like when people aren't talking polite enough. Same as Mom." Geneva steps closer to the window, and a breeze catches a wave of her heavy brown hair. Her mouth is a sealed smile, and her fingers—usually knotted together or jammed under her arms to protect her from stray germs—gently press against the outline of her jaw as she leans out, breathing the spring air. It is not a Geneva thing to do, considering she often refers to breezes as drafts.

"You okay?"

"I feel good." Geneva's voice is soft and

confiding. "This afternoon wasn't so bad after all, in fact it makes me think . . ."

Only she loses her thought to the fresh air, stretching herself deeper out the window and letting the wind smooth over her face.

the other shepards

"So clean and smooth." Brett raises his wine glass and tilts it. The liquid inside catches an identical shade of light from the chandelier.

"Like springtime," Carla adds. At the other end of the table, Mom nods and raises her own glass.

"Cheers to spring," she says. Dad picks up his glass. Geneva and I reach for our water goblets, and I make a silent bet. *If you can count to one hundred in a single breath, then baby Freddie will wake up and you can be excused to take care of him.*

"And to the ides of March, and Lydia's fifty-sixth," Dad adds. *Clink, clink.* Geneva's heavy water goblet tips dangerously. I take a huge breath and start counting, *one, two, three . . .*

The vase has been presented, air kisses exchanged. We brought out and unrolled the vellum paper, too, and explained our choices for what Geneva calls the "birds of paradise" design. Mom looks surprised by the idea of painting a mural in the kitchen. Her face is quizzical but guarded. She stares across the table at Dad and mouths secret sentences to him, something she would not normally do because she considers it impolite.

"This is a big project," Dad says to me with a funny, freeze-dried smile after viewing the sketch selection.

"Annie's a professional artist."

"You girls seem very excited."

"She says we can help. She says she'll be the supervisor."

"Ah." He winks at me, a wink that seems filled with conspiracy, and I am struck by the idea that perhaps Annie is not an artist after all. Maybe Dad has hired another psychiatrist to try to help Geneva.

My sister has been in and out of therapy ever since she could crawl. Holidays are often recalled as they coincided with Geneva's phobias and compulsions. 'Was that the Thanksgiving that Geneva had to floss her teeth ten times a day because she got fixated on tartar?' 'Remember, it was the same summer that Geneva had to line up everybody's shoes in a row before she could go to sleep.' The occasional bouts with counseling never seem to do anything to change her, but the parents like to get updates on her psyche from time to time.

Annie the undercover therapist. The plan makes sense, especially in light of the parents' subdued and slightly mortified approach to Geneva's problems.

"She knows a lot about art. She's going to transform the kitchen," I gasp, trying not to lose too much air, while my fingers keep count—*fourteen, fifteen, sixteen*—and I wink back at Dad.

"We almost never use the kitchen," Mom says in an explaining, slightly ashamed way to Carla. "I think it's a hint that the girls are trying to get more home cooking out of me." Suddenly it occurs to me that Mom might not want the kitchen mural.

"It'll be beautiful," I promise, but Mom's answering smile does not erase the concern from her eyes.

"We're going to help Annie every afternoon." Geneva lifts her eyes from her slice of birthday cake as she speaks. Her sudden connection to the table is jarring. Even the usually dignified Carla looks startled as Geneva starts talking about paint primers and chalk outlines.

After she is finished no one says a word; it is that shocking. Then Brett clears his throat and begins telling the parents about his job.

The odorless tulips block my view. I stretch my neck and stare giraffelike over the leaves, trying to slide Brett's face back in time, into its firm, seventeen-year-old shape. *Thirty, thirty-one, thirty-two . . .*

"I see you, Peeper." Brett grins at me, interrupting himself a moment from talking about how he expects to be made full associate at the bank by next year. He has movie-star teeth, white as new sneakers. His other, real teeth all got smashed out long ago, the night Kevin's jeep flipped. Brett's entire jaw had to be rewired. You can clearly see the scar from where his bottom teeth ripped through the skin of his chin just below his lip. The brambly pink etching of scar tissue helps his chipmunk face look tough, even mysterious, like a Man with a Past.

In photographs of teenage Brett, he is a tender ugly duckling, flanked by my two grinning, handsome-and-know-it brothers. It always seems strange to me that not only was Brett the one person to survive that night, but between his false teeth and his dashing pirate's scar he actually emerged from the accident somewhat improved. A poisonous thought, Mom would say. Not that I'd ever mention it out loud.

Baby Freddie, please cry! My breath is beginning to run out. *Forty-six, forty-seven, forty-eight.* Distract yourself.

"It's hard to believe the years have passed so quickly," Mom is commenting. "And now you, Brett, with your family, and about to be named full associate. Time marches on, doesn't it, Quentin?"

My father's eyes are dark, dry raisins, half-buried in the gentle pleats of his skin. My mother's eyes are glassy with a liquid that never spills. They stare across the dining room table, holding each other in private memories.

Freddie must be sleeping soundly. *Fifty-nine, sixty, sixty-one* . . . forget it. Breath burps from my lungs with a *phof!* and Dad looks over at me.

"You and your sister are excused from the table," he says. I smile; I won my bet after all.

Geneva plunks down her water, bolts up from her chair, and motors out of the dining room and up the stairs so fast that the liquid is still shifting back and forth in her goblet when we hear her bedroom door slam. That was rude, Mom will reprimand her later, not to say good night to our guests. I know Mom wants me to linger to make up for Geneva. And so I stay, although Mom's next sentence makes me wish that I had disappeared while I had the opportunity.

"Holland, I meant to tell you. I ran into Angie Hill this afternoon." *Blech*—Mrs. Hill. The only woman on the planet known to have given birth to a night crawler, now age fourteen and a freshman at Bishop Brown High School, which must have a relaxed policy on admitting night crawlers.

"Oh, really?" I smile politely and hope Mom is not leading up to a mention of Aaron. No such luck. "She told me that Aaron wasn't going to fencing camp, and so they'll all be down at the shore this summer. They're renting on Bayberry, one road over from us, during the same two weeks that we're there. Isn't that fun?"

"Yes, I guess, except that Aaron and me—"

"Aaron and I."

"Aaron and I aren't exactly as good friends as we were when we were little kids," I say, remembering last Christmas, when the Hills came over and Aaron, as a kind of nonfunny joke, kept calling me his "kissing cousin" and tried to drag me under the mistletoe. Both sets of parents had laughed indulgently, and I'd finally let him plant one on my cheek. His gooey lips slid like a worm across my skin, and that's when I privately had rechristened Aaron.

"No," Mom corrects my opinion. "You forget how well the two of you get along, because you don't spend enough time together anymore. Remember that game, that unicorn game you both made up on the merry-go-round in Central Park? You two loved that game. It was all Angie and I could do to pull you off those horses." There is laughter from every mouth at the table except mine.

"That was in second grade," I say, annoyed. "But sure, I guess it'll be nice to have Aaron around this summer." The dutiful daughter. Mom smiles and I know I have won her favor.

"It was awesome to see you both, Brett and Carla. And if you ever want me to baby-sit Freddie, I'd like to. Anytime." I circle the table, careful not to be the bluebird of Ickness, no kissing and hugging anyone too hard, although Brett's aftershave is wonderful and spicy. "Happy Birthday, Mom. Good night, everyone." Mom is still smiling. A job well done: not too abrupt, not too straggly, just enough sweetness.

"She's very dear," Carla says after I have left the dining room and am walking up the stairs.

"Holland, thankfully, does not cause us a moment's worry." Dad's voice is loud from wine, and I stop, not breathing, a hand squeezing each banister. "Responsible, and she's smart as a whip. She did the most extraordinary science project last semester on human cell division. The diorama's still in the den, if you want to have a look. Meiosis, mitosis, mitochondria . . . She made the vacuoles out of hair gel and sandwich baggies. Pretty clever, eh?"

"A head for science, just like her old man." Brett's voice. Then Dad again, even louder.

"I'm going to try to get her a summer internship at the University. I've started on the paperwork. I don't anticipate a problem. High honors in science on her report card every . . ."

I run up the stairs, suddenly conscious of my eavesdropping, and yet tingling with anger. I had no idea about a summer internship, or that Dad had taken my science project this seriously. It is just like my father, though, to plan my life behind my back and then spring it on me. I'll have to figure out a countermaneuver, maybe start looking into summer jobs or camps. What could be worse than spending my vacation hunched over a Bunsen burner? Just because I'm good in science does not mean I like it.

Baby Freddie is snoring itty-bitty baby snores from inside the Port-o-Crib that Carla set up in Dad's study. I bend to whisper good night and catch a scent of his skin. I can't ever remember baby Geneva smelling so fresh. I always imagine us both born slightly dried and crumbled, like cheddar cheese, prewrapped in musty hand-me-down nightgowns. No, we could never have been like Freddie, so new and soft and thoughtless.

I run a finger over the downy fold of baby Freddie's neck and listen to his breathing, a lispy lullaby that draws my eyelids closed. I better start my French verbs. Geneva stayed in the kitchen today because of my bet, and I never break my bets. It's not the kind of risk I take.

Late that night, I wake to the sound of my name. I rise from my bed and pad across the hall to Geneva's room. She sits bolt upright, all sleep-shadowed eyes and sleep-prickly hair.

"Another dream?" I ask.

"It was for real. I keep telling you. They were here."

"Tell me again," I whisper, sliding onto the edge of her bed. My just-awakened body bends awkwardly, and I crook my fingers over my cold toes.

"Geneva?" Mom's thin silhouette outlines the doorway. In the darkness, dressed in her slippers and robe, she looks more frail than by daylight, when she is outfitted for work in one of her neutral suits and knotted silk scarves.

"She had a bad dream about Elizabeth and John and Kevin," I tell her. "She's fine now."

"But they mustn't ever be a bad dream," Mom chides us mildly. "They're angels now, watching over you girls and protecting you. Your brothers and sister love you both so dearly."

"They stood in my room, and they told me...," the quick, warning shift of Mom's body makes Geneva hesitate, "that they were in heaven with God and all the archangels and they miss us. But heaven has lots of sunsets and they're very happy."

"Well, that doesn't sound like a bad dream," Mom says. "To me, that sounds like a very nice visit from your family."

"Visiting hours are over," Geneva mumbles, her voice too small for Mom to hear.

"I'll stay with her," I say. "Don't worry about us. Get some sleep."

"You're a love, Holland. Good night, girls."

Mom closes the door quickly, as if I suddenly might change my mind. Geneva's nocturnal visions lost their punch years ago, when we realized they could not be cured except by the nightly sedatives prescribed by our family psychiatrist, Dr. Bushnell, which left us with a Geneva so groggy that she could barely put her shoes on the right feet the next morning. When she was taken off the pills, the dreams resumed. "Just leave her" was Dr. Bushnell's next piece of advice. "Like a baby who must learn to stop crying. Just leave her and eventually she will sleep through the night."

Mom and Dad seemed to have appreciated this suggestion, and now it is rare for them to respond to Geneva. Maybe they do not even hear her anymore, since she only calls my name. But to me, Geneva's voice is as harsh as a dog whistle, claiming me from anywhere, forcing me to run and fetch and stay. Sometimes, she has admitted, she calls out to me for no other reason than to make sure that I am here, that I will come.

"You need a bath?" I ask. "Would water fix you?"

She doesn't answer, just pushes out from under her blankets and thumps her feet on the floor.

"Shhh."

"Who cares?" She sniffs. "Who hears?"

"Shhh," I repeat. I follow her out to the hall and into the bathroom. Geneva is not modest; she sheds her nightgown and underpants while I run the faucet, then sinks cautiously into the tub, slowly allowing the steam and hot water to envelop her.

"Bubbles, please," she yawns. I fetch the bottle from under the sink and pour a trickle of purple slime into the stream.

"Tell me," I say. "You haven't dreamt about them in a while."

"It's real, Holland, more real than dreaming. I could see them." Geneva looks at me with eyes syrupy from the heat. "They walked into my room and they seemed so regular, just like in their pictures. They were all wearing jeans. Kevin had on a green windbreaker. John said, 'Wake up, Neeve,' which is strange, now that I think about it, because nobody calls me that. Except for it seemed normal." She pauses. "Then Elizabeth said, 'You're in my dreams, too, Neeve.'"

"And?" I try not to sound too interested, but my inner eye becomes fixed on this image. I watch their shadows jag across Geneva's wall. Their faces flicker in the glow of Geneva's night light. The shells of their jackets are damp with salt water. I can smell the spearmint crackle of their chewing gum, see the spritz of freckles on

Kevin's nose. "Wake up," John whispers. I shudder. For a moment it is as if my sister's dream has dissolved into my own consciousness.

"And nothing. That was the end."

I turn off the water and sit down on the closed toilet seat. "Dreams are easy to explain," I begin in a ponderous voice like a PBS narrator. "A dream is like a garbage disposal of things that happen in your day, which get mashed up and pushed through your sleeping mind. The nights Brett comes over are kind of upsetting because he makes us think about Elizabeth and the boys, and how they can't be with us."

"I guess," she says, nodding. Her wet hair pastes to her shoulders like flattened threads of brown cotton. Surrounded by bubbles and light, she looks more sweet and agreeable than she did a few minutes ago. "It's been a while since I wanted to see them."

"Aha. See what you said? You want to see them, so your mind makes up a story."

"But you don't?"

"Don't what?"

"Want to see them?"

"Of course I do," I answer, "but it's an impossible wish. I mean, I've never even seen the mayor, and half the neighborhood's spotted him."

"That's because you need me to show you where to look," Geneva says. "My eyes work better than yours."

I ignore her remark, moving my seat to kneel on the bath mat, and I sink a washcloth into the warm water, spreading it over her curled, spiny back. "Come on, let's wash you up so we can get back to bed."

"Everything would be different if they were here. Imagine if they had been sitting with us at the table tonight, helping Mom celebrate."

"If the other Shepards had been here tonight," I say lightly, "there wouldn't be room for us at the table." Although she nods in agreement, Geneva's arms tighten around her knees.

"Holland, do you remember when we were little, how we made up that imaginary friend, Nonie, who lived under the dining room table?"

"Sure I do." She had been our secret friend for years. I had been upset when eventually I grew too big to squeeze under the table to play. "She liked to eat your vegetables, and once you got mad at Uncle Nelson for accidentally kicking her."

"See, that's how it was tonight. Like visits from imaginary friends." Geneva grabs around for the washcloth, dunks it, and presses it over her face. "Only they didn't have to leave so quick," she says, her voice not so muffled that I can't hear the fierceness in it.

"I think Annie made a good point this afternoon. I bet Kevin and Elizabeth and John would be unhappy to know that the only time we ever talk about them are in depressing conversations like this."

"Annie also said that Mom and Dad are lucky to have us." Geneva's washcloth mask drops to reveal her blotchy face as she stands up in the tub. I hold her hand as she wobbles, dripping, onto the bath mat, where I wrap her up like a burrito in a king-size towel. "Which proves Annie doesn't know everything. I bet sometimes Mom and Dad wish we would go away. They only want to be with each other. We were a bad idea—they're too old to have our-age kids in the house. They'd be better off being grandparents, seeing us for visits. They're as old as grandparents, anyway."

"That's not fair to Mom and Dad," I reprove. "They're better than most Ambrose parents; they come to all our school recitals, they care about our grades and what we eat and if we're wearing our bike helmets, all that stuff. We're the lucky ones, really, to have parents like them.

Now dry off and give me your towel. I'll meet you back in your room."

She dries and scoots, streaking across the hall while I arrange the damp towel over the rack and then rinse the bathtub of bubble residue.

Alone, I think hard about what Geneva has said, but even as I reexamine her words, I want to throw them away. It reminds me of an afternoon, years ago, when we sneaked a box of slides marked ST. G—NEW YEAR out of Dad's study. The parents were not home, but we ran into my bedroom and locked the door anyway. I remember that we were laughing, that my heart was beating on hummingbirds' wings. At first the theft seemed so tantalizing.

Geneva would hold up a slide to my bedside table lamp, squint at it, then pass it to me. The images were tiny, but imprinted themselves permanently on my strained and hungry eyes. Mom squished between the boys. The whole family piled up on a hammock. Elizabeth eating a cheeseburger. The box contained over a hundred slides, and we examined each one with scientific intensity. When we were finished, Geneva said disgustedly, "I knew it. The parents used up all the love on them." Her words had terrified me into never forgetting them, and

I realized that in part she was right. The other Shepards were Ick. They overloved. That day, I felt as if my sister and I had been betrayed.

I tried not to dwell on the betrayal or the pictures after that, although from time to time I've been back in the study and sneaked out batches of slides, like greedy handfuls of after dinner mints, to savor privately in my room. But I don't think my sister ever looked at another slide again.

When I meet Geneva back in her room, she has changed into fresh pajamas and is in bed, almost asleep.

"Stay," she implores, catching my sleeve. "While I say prayers."

"Okay. Then do you want me to sing?"

"Yuck, no. Will you check my throat for swollen glands?"

I check. Her neck is smooth as usual. Geneva got swollen glands about a year and a half ago, and ever since then she has been anxiously waiting for a recurrence.

"Nope."

She folds her hands together and tucks them under her cheek, an angelic sleeping position she copied from an Olsen twins movie, and she races twice through the Our Father so fast that the words break up funny—"earth asitisin heaven."

"Slow down," I whisper. "You don't even hear what you're saying."

She pays no attention. Her third time through, Geneva loses speed and yawns. She only gets past two lines of the fourth round, but I sit a while longer to make sure she is not dreaming.

louis littlebird

Louis Littlebird is standing on line at the coffee vendor parked on the curb of Fourteenth Street and Sixth Avenue. It is early and I am tired, although I had been following my daily bet of walking on the left side of even-numbered streets and on the right side of odd-numbered streets in a hopeful exchange for finding him.

This morning my bet finally worked, and I have made Louis appear. His bleach-blond and normal-brown hair is a pattern of stripes as identifying as a flag. Closer, I see that he wears his leather jacket over a sage green sweatshirt stamped with the letters BBHS and that he has on his motorcycle boots.

"I want coffee," I tell Geneva. I speed my pace and glance at my reflection in the glass double doors of an apartment building. The reflected girl holds her book bag too high on her back, and her chin leads the rest of her body. I stop and realign myself, allowing my hips to take the lead and loosening my grip on my bag, although now its more casually arranged weight seems heavier.

"Coffee before school?" Geneva squeaks. "Annie's already got you addicted. Hey, you think she might come back this afternoon? She said she was coming. She has to, right? Right?"

I grope for the lunch money in my coat pocket. Louis turns as Geneva's voice drifts into earshot, and I know he sees us by the way he squints to a place just left of my head, then looks away. He has already bought breakfast: a carton of juice and a doughnut blanketed in coconut choppings. But he won't go yet, up the street and across a block to Bishop Brown High School, where he is a freshman in the same class as the night crawler. Now that Louis has seen me, I know he won't go.

Louis slides his backpack off his shoulder, then kneels down beside it to unzip one of the compartments. I watch him with the attention of a scout reporter covering my first story.

I stroll up to the vendor, Geneva in tow.

"One small coffee, one small orange juice," I order. "And a cruller. To split." I turn to Geneva. "Okay?"

"But I wanted coffee, too," she whines.

"I'm older, I'm allowed to have breakfast coffee."

"Besides, it'll stunt your growth," Louis says, standing up and stepping toward us.

"Hi," says Geneva, looking at Louis and trying to place him. She does not know that I have been on constant Louis watch since the afternoon we met him, nearly two months ago. She does not know that, when I learned that he commutes to his school from Carroll Gardens, in Brooklyn, I calculated he would take the F train—which stops at Fourteenth and Sixth—and head east. She does not know that I altered the course of our own route to school so that we cross on Fourteenth Street, even though our school is one street below and we always have to walk down again. She does not realize that for the past two months we have been leaving home up to twenty minutes early or late for school as part of my ongoing experiment to synchronize our commute with Louis Littlebird's.

"Hey, I remember now," Geneva says. "We met you in January at the Sam Flax, when we were buying book cover paper. We helped you find paint for your posters."

"Uh-huh," Louis answers. He tears off the end of his straw wrapper and spits it into the wind.

"Litter!" Geneva races after the blowing paper. Louis and I watch her spring down the sidewalk, chasing it.

"Strung like a fiddle," Louis says. "Your sister's wired. Same as that day in Sam Flax, saying she would throw up if she couldn't use the employee bathroom. I remember. She doesn't need caffeine, that's for sure." He looks at me and I tilt my head and sip my coffee, petrified by the knowledge that after the cup leaves my lips, I will have to think of something to say and I have no idea what.

Meanwhile, my brain is snapping hundreds of tiny pictures. Louis's skin is olive dark, there's a mole just beside his right eyebrow, he's traded the black stud for a gold hoop in his left ear, his wrestler's shoulders are wide and sloped and thick. I would give my whole allowance at this moment to put my hands on those shoulders. Very Ick, Mom would say.

"What time is it?" I ask. Dumb question, obvious, stupid.

"A little past eight."

"Oh, did those posters come out right? Those ones for your wrestling team?" Better. Louis smiles and swigs his juice.

"Yeah, great. The glow-in-the-dark paint looked so pro. We had a lot of people show up to support the team. I won my weight division, too. You should have come and watched. There was enough room in the stands. You said you'd be there."

"Um, sorry about that." Except that I *was* there, up in the way, way back bleachers. I watched Louis Littlebird wrestle and pin his opponent in the 145-pound category. Afterward, I chickened out and ran home. But what was I supposed to do, run up to him, tousle his hair, and smack his backside, along with the rest of his teammates? "I'll come to the next one, I promise."

"Season's over. We're in baseball tryouts now."

Geneva bounds up. "I threw it away in the trash," she announces. "Come on, Holland, you said if we had time we could stop at Piza Ricemann. Hey, I just thought, it seems stupid for us to walk all the way up here, we're double-walking a block somewhere, aren't we? I bet it would be faster—"

"Okay, let's go then." I nudge Geneva not so gently.

"Wait." Louis takes an uncertain step closer to us, then drops back. "You go to Monsignor Ambrose, right?"

"Yeah."

"You're Catholic, or you just go there?"

"Catholic when I feel like it."

Louis wrinkles his nose. "Is that a joke?"

I shrug, but the air between us suddenly bristles with tension. "Why, are you seriously religious or something?"

"I gave up beating on my kid brother for Lent," he says. "That's serious."

"I gave up candy," I counter. "My sister did, too. But we're not, you know, obsessed with it. We don't go to church camp or anything."

"I did not give up candy," Geneva says. "I didn't give up anything this year. Mom explained it was a personal decision. So I decided there's still too much stuff I personally am not allowed to do, and God would understand that I can't afford to sacrifice more." Louis laughs, and I relax slightly.

"Your name's like Ireland or something."

"Holland."

"Uh-huh. I remember. Some strange-ass name."

"That is called swearing," Geneva says.

"An ass is a donkey," Louis says gravely, raising his hand. "Gotta rock. Take care," he says.

"Bye." I turn quickly so that we can leave him before he leaves us.

"Your face is red," Geneva squawks. "Why is your face so red? Did you really give up candy?"

"Would you be quiet?" I growl. I abandon my slow, hips-first walk as I jostle Geneva down the sidewalk.

"What, do you like him or something? He looks like an acid-house-music kid, like Sophie's brother. Get your hand off my neck!"

"Come on, we'll be late."

"We will not. We left fifteen minutes early today. You like him, I can tell. He looks like a rebel. Mom would never let him come over in that leather jacket and with that partly white hair. She would call him an unprincipled thug. I mean it, stop hurting me! What's wrong with you today?"

"What's wrong with *you*? Calling him a litterbug! Yelling at him for swearing! Being an obnoxious little sister, after all I did last night, giving you a bath and staying with you after your boring blah blah blah nightmare."

In the silence that follows my skin chills with my own cruelty. How hateful, Mom would say. What an unthinking, poisonous sister. What *is* wrong with you, Holland? Yet I remain stubborn, yanking Geneva's hand at the cross lights and, even more hurtfully, refusing to comment on or even to stop at the freshly draped and sequined mannequin display in the window of Piza Ricemann. Geneva *needs* to know that you are angry, another part of me argues.

Most of my thoughts are not really focused on Geneva at all. I found him, trumpets the loudest, most victorious inside voice. I hunted him down, and today I found out exactly when and exactly how Louis Littlebird gets to school in the morning.

We stop outside the side entrance of Ambrose, at the yellow door where we always part for the day.

"Pick you up at 3:10," I say. "Sorry I was a grouch earlier." Geneva does not answer and when I look at her, I see that her face is teary. I defrost and melt in an instant, folding my arms over her shoulders.

"Look, I'm sorry, please don't cry. I am so—" But Geneva pushes solidly from my grip.

"Go drown yourself," she hisses. She turns and is lapped up into the wave of sixth graders rushing through the door.

"Aw, come on. I said I'm sorry," I call after her. I stand, undecided, but then I turn and head toward the eighth grade doors. Let her go.

In homeroom, I add to my list in the back of my notebook under the heading: More Facts About L. L.

    24. Swears

    25. Possib. house music?

    26. Brown eyes (not black, like you thought!) with small goldeny dots around pupils

    27. Younger brother

    28. Catholic

    29. Litters

    30. Gold hoop earring

    31. Breakfast/vendor @ 8:05–8:10 A.M.!!!

At the sound of the attendance bell I bat my book shut and swipe it into my desk, banging the top down, but it is more difficult for me to put away my thoughts. The Louis I bumped into this morning was a more earnest, less detached guy than the one I met in the Sam Flax. I will have to readjust my daydreams, give him a softer approach when we have imaginary conversations or when he asks me out on pretend dates.

I spread my fingers over the desk's surface and pretend that I am touching Louis Littlebird's face. My fingertips are damp against his skin, the hollows beneath his eyes, the raised notch of his throat. The top of my desk feels warm, as if my notebook is heating its surface from the inside like a rising, bubbling dessert.

"Mrs. Garcia, will you please send Holland Shepard to the front desk," the secretary's voice burrs through the intercom. Geneva.

"Uh-oh, Holland's gonna get it."

"Hollandaise is in trou-ble."

"Go girl, go girl."

"Betcha it's bad baby sis again."

I stand up and look at Mrs. Garcia, who dismisses me with her hand. I cannot resist grabbing my notebook, dangerous with its unprotected secrets.

Habit sends me strolling past the front desk and the principal's office and straight to the nurse's station. Geneva lies coiled on a high iron cot. She has ripped off a corner of the sterile, germ-catching paper strip that covers the pillow and is twisting it in her hands. Her pale legs are blue and goose-bumped in the uncovered space between her knee socks and her kilt. Mrs. Just, the school nurse, smiles at me but she looks irritated.

"Here's a pickle," she says. "Can you do anything, or should I give her one of her pills? I sure did not count on this today, no sirree."

"Geneva, what is it?" I whisper in her ear. "What's freaking you out now?" I smooth her hair away from her face and try to press one of her hands into mine so that she will stop her paper twisting. "You're being very dramatic," I say. "How can I help you without knowing what's bothering you?"

"When I said for you to drown yourself."

"Who? Who?" Mrs. Just hoots. "Who's drowning?" Geneva's two front teeth clamp to lock over her bottom lip.

"I know you didn't mean it, silly." I talk in our secret voice. "People always say things they don't mean when they're angry."

"I closed my eyes and I saw you drowned like in the story of Joseph of Canaan, who got pushed down the well by his mean brothers. I called down the well but there was no answer. You were drowned, and it was all my fault."

"That's very horrible." I sigh. Mrs. Just wrinkles her nose.

"As I recall, Joseph didn't drown in the well," she says with a sniff. "To my memory, Juda pulled him out, and he and his brothers sold Joseph to merchants for twenty pieces of silver."

"I would never sell you to merchants, Holland," Geneva vows.

"Geneva, get hold of yourself." I pat her arm. "You're working yourself up over nothing."

"I hate this day. I want a new day." She squeezes herself into a tighter knot and pulls her hair over her face. All I see is an island of nose. "I want to go home."

"Home?" Mrs. Just looks at me. "Home? There's no need for that. I can call one of your parents to see if she can take a calm-down pill from her prescription. I'm telling you if she's got one of her pills, then she can rest here through the morning and won't miss afternoon classes."

"Sure," I agree.

"This day is wrecked," Geneva whines. "I'm going home. I want another day."

Mrs. Just licks a finger for every page she flips of Geneva's thick medical record. She moves over to her desk, reaching for the telephone.

"Mom will be upset to hear this," I say. "Dad, too. They'll give you that talk about leaders of tomorrow."

"I feel dizzy. I might throw up. You were so mean to me this morning, Holland. It put snakes in my stomach."

"You shouldn't give me so much power that

I could send you into such a tailspin." I try not to sound too much like Mom.

"My nightmares are not dumb or little, like you said. They're real. They're more real to me than today is."

"Oh, give me a break." I look at Geneva's nose and fight an urge to pinch it. I am impatient with the same old hatful of Geneva's tricks, but I am angry at myself for thinking that her scenes are anything she can help.

"She's asking to talk to one of you." Mrs. Just sets down the receiver and looks crossly from me to Geneva. I reach for the phone.

"Mom?"

"I can't deal with this right now, Holland. The people from Riverside are here."

"So what do you want me to do?"

"What does she want?"

"To go home, of course."

"Will you put her on?"

The only words Geneva says after I hand her the phone are that she is going home right now, that she has snakes in her stomach, and that she wants a new day. I am back on the line in less than a minute.

"Could you just walk her back?" Mom sounds defeated. Geneva has that effect. "Today of all days, it's impossible . . ."

"And then what?"

"And then I'll leave here early, as soon as I can get out. I'll call you at home and let you know when I'm coming. All right?" I make a grumpy sound of agreement. Mom sighs. "Thank you. And you know how I hate for you to miss school, but this is the one day I absolutely cannot—"

"Don't worry about it, Mom."

"Thank you, really, Holland, I don't know where I'd be. Now would you put Mrs. Just back on?"

I pass the phone to Mrs. Just as Geneva uncurls and squirms off the cot. She knows she has won. "I'll meet you outside," she informs me, her voice no more than a puff of triumph as she sweeps out the door. I wait for Mrs. Just to finish the call. She hangs up in a huff, obviously annoyed.

"Your mom told me to go ahead and write up the excuse notes for Sister Nuella."

"Thanks, Mrs. Just. I'll stop off in homeroom to tell Mrs. Garcia we're going, and to get my assignments."

"Know what I think?" Mrs. Just's expression is severe, and she presses her hand over her heart as if she is about to start angrily reciting the Pledge of Allegiance. I wait, listening. "I think Missie's got your whole family wrapped around her little finger. You're a good girl, Holland. You're never in here moaning for aspirins or sick notes or going on about cramps. But look at you, pulled out of school because your sister's having another fit, and your mom knows someone's got to take care of her. It's plain as pie to me that all Missie needs is a good spanking. She wouldn't be allowed to play the little queenie in my house, I'm telling you now. I'm saying that in my home, playing possum'd last under three seconds—"

"You're right, you're right," I say. It's all I know to say to a speech I've heard too many times before. "But still, I'd better go."

I collect my things from homeroom and meet Geneva outside. She greets me with a feeble smirk.

"Mom is going to pack you off to a special school," I say. "A school for the seriously disturbed and spoiled." Geneva starts walking, ignoring me.

"By the way, I'm going back to Ambrose, after I drop you off. This is ridiculous. Mom either should have come for you herself or made you stay in school. I'm not your service bureau of transportation." I kick a discarded apple core into her path. "There, there's some more litter to throw away, since you're so interested in the environment lately."

"Fruit is biodegradable," she says. "Get the facts."

I clench my hands, I want to pull out her hair so badly. It is too much, sometimes, always being the older one, the unpaid baby-sitter and nursemaid for a thankless little sister.

We keep silent until we turn onto our street. Geneva picks up speed, her purposeful walk turning into a brisk skip, and her throat catches in a small, pleased sound. I look at her, mystified by the smile that transfixes her face, then the jackrabbiting bounds that carry her through the home stretch to our front door. I don't understand what could get her so animated.

And then, at once, I do.

geneva and annie

"Girls!" We stop at the echo of her voice, a hollow boomerang down the walled alley. Annie's hair blows sideways across her face in a tangled puff as she leans dangerously far out the kitchen window. "What brings you two out of school?"

"We knew you'd be here!" Geneva runs around to the front of the house and jets inside the front door. I follow her into the kitchen. Annie already is pulling down the coffee mugs.

"Who's sick?" she asks. "Neither of you looks it."

"We're having a hooky day," Geneva gloats.

"Everybody needs one sometime," Annie says, her smile untroubled, although I can't imagine what she must think of my delinquent sister.

"You're supposed to have a stomachache," I reprimand her. "Otherwise I'm calling Mom." I look at Annie. "Maybe I should phone her anyway," I say. "Since you're here, would you mind keeping an eye on Geneva while I go back to school?" My question is matter-of-fact, but my body does not make any effort to move me to the phone in the front hall.

"If she doesn't mind helping me," Annie says. Geneva has already kicked off her shoes and is paging through the art books. "Coffee before you set out again, weary traveler?" Annie's eyes are two gentle lights shining over her mug. I notice that her makeup is more smeared than yesterday, she wears the same strappy shoes and linen blazer, and the messy knot of her hair is lopsided, as if she might have spent last night sleeping on a park bench. She smells nice, though, like crayons or chalk.

"A little mess is legal as long as there's no evidence of dirt," Mom once said to me in a conversation about straightening up my bedroom. That is Annie today. Messy not dirty.

She pours out a mug, which I accept. I had not felt weary until she used the word; maybe the coffee will pep me up. Except that Annie's blend seems to work an opposite effect—its smell and taste are mellow, and thoughts of returning to school begin to tumble away from me.

"I was planning to go downtown after I finished priming," Annie tells us. "If you girls want to join me, I'd be glad for the company."

"We aren't allowed to wander around the city without permission," I explain in as polite a voice as I know. Geneva gives me a black look.

"I'm supervising, remember, so I grant permission," Annie says. "I grew up in this city, and I was queen of the baby-sitters here for years. It was how I made all my clothes money. My mom hated my taste in clothes. She wanted to dress me like a doll, I guess since I was her only girl, but I wanted cool stuff like velour pants and satin ice-skate skirts, and my mom refused to buy it. She would say things like, 'Clothing that disintegrates in two weeks' time isn't worth the hanger it's hung on.'"

I smile and nod; it sounds just like something Mom would say.

"Our mom never buys us velour or satin anything," Geneva says admiringly. "Even if it's on a one-day, seventy-five-percent-off sale at Macy's."

"You'll find any costume you want at the thrift stores."

"But today is a school day," I say. "Maybe we shouldn't go downtown, where everyone can see us not being in school."

"Believe me, no one will care, as long as you act reasonably mature," Annie says. "And you both look too old to do the really idiotic kid stuff, like drink bleach or hide granola in the VCR. I baby-sat a girl once who did that. It was trouble, because her big brother, Marty, was a karate video addict. After she messed up the video machine with granola, there was nothing for Marty to watch.

"He was eight years old, and I had to get him addicted to the soap operas, which took a pretty good trick. You know how you instantly get an eight-year-old boy addicted to soap operas?" Annie looks at us, savoring the moment. "Tell him that it's all really happening, all real life, in the apartment upstairs!" Annie laughs her hiccuping laugh, and I exhale a sigh of appreciation. You don't hear a good baby-sitting trick every day.

Under the table, Geneva gives my shoe a gentle kick. I look over at her and nod, and she grins. She knows how much I want to hand Annie the controls of the day. Why wouldn't I? It'd be more fun than other versions of this morning, trying to memorize irregular French verbs or holding Geneva's hand in the nurse's station.

We finish breakfast and then go up to our rooms to change into jeans and sweatshirts, "slop-around clothes," as Annie instructs. After changing, Geneva dashes back to the kitchen, but I detour through the second floor, drifting into rooms. The grandfather clock in the den chimes ten elegant, muted strokes, but time feels enchanted, as if this particular morning has been scooped up from the precise march of minutes and hours of a normal school day.

I follow the carpet runner, betting myself. *If you can walk on the balls of your feet into every room on the second floor without losing balance, then Mom will let you and Geneva stay home from school with Annie the whole day.*

Our townhouse is tall and narrow, a three-story stack of dark rooms, some of which have no real function and are referred to with vague names such as "the sitting room," "the yellow room," or "the Korean chest room." This last room, at the far end of the second-floor stairs, was where Elizabeth slept. At the other end of the hall stand Kevin and John's old bedrooms, facing each other across the landing, the bathroom and linen closet between them.

I bounce through John's room, then Kevin's, my toes spread and crooked like a bird's for balance. Both rooms are arranged into informal studies, with bookshelves and armchairs, but since all of us prefer using the downstairs den, which has the computer and television, the rooms are dusty with disuse. When I sneeze, my heels almost drop to the floor; I recover just in time. I look at the ceiling, to the triangle of Kevin's Greek alphabet Delta he painted up there when he got into his top choice fraternity. "A guy's guy" is how Brett always describes Kevin. An athlete, a daredevil, a leader. "Not much of a student but a lot of fun." John was quieter, but Brett said he could imitate sounds: bird calls, the crash of thunder, anything. It helped him out for practical jokes. "They loved a good joke, those two," Brett told me. "John was brainy and Kevin was bold. And Elizabeth knew how to laugh off both of 'em."

It is nearly impossible to imagine those types of people living in this silent house.

I glide on the balls of my feet, ankles cracking with my unaccustomed shift of weight, into the Korean chest room, where there is no

Korean chest because five or six years ago Mom gave it away to my Uncle Nelson as a Christmas present, "so that he'd stop embarrassing both of us with all that obscene hinting."

Elizabeth's desk is the only piece of the room that has remained the same from the time she lived here. I tiptoe toward it. More than any photo or anecdote, this desk, with its surface of baby blue painted wood, imprinted with a Led Zeppelin sticker and scratchwork heart bearing the initials E. S. + W. J., makes me feel close to the sister I never knew.

When Mom shipped out the Korean chest, she impulsively had the room freshly wallpapered in a green pattern that looks like battle lines of asparagus, and carpeted with a cream-of-tomato red rug. She then bought a pull-out futon, moving it into the space the chest had occupied. "Now you girls can have guests sleep over in here," she explained, answering the question Geneva and I had been silently asking during those weeks of frantic redecorating. "It's very modern and charming now."

"Friends to lure onto the spooky second floor of 176 Waverly," Geneva had said smirking.

"If you can stay the whole night you get a bag of gold," I added. "Mom must have got her redecorating idea straight from Dr. Bushnell.

He's always saying how we have to move away from the other Shepards. Maybe this is Mom's way of moving."

It's hard to leave behind the other family, though, especially since their story is common knowledge in our school. Elizabeth herself was a student at Ambrose, so there are teachers who remember her, and returning alumnae seem to feel duty bound to tell me about how they knew Elizabeth in some small way.

There is even the annually given Elizabeth A. Shepard plaque for Excellence in Tennis and Sportsmanship. Mom presents it every year at the school's seventh grade commencement. I won it last year, although it probably should have gone to Moira Radcovich. I play a decent game of tennis, but nothing special. Mom had hugged me on stage, in front of the entire sixth, seventh, and eighth grades. It had been a horrible day, not only because I was completely unprepared for Mom's outburst of Ick, but because every single clapping hand in that auditorium knew the same thing: those Shepards are still kind of a mess.

"Holland, what are you doing?" Geneva hollers from the kitchen, which is just beneath Elizabeth's room. "I hear you bumping around up there! We're starting to talk about painting."

"Coming!" The scent of coffee is powerful, drifting up through the vent. They must be brewing another pot.

The top of Elizabeth's desk is furry with dust. I trace long, swirling letters through it, bravely spelling out Louis Littlebird. Each L rolls deliciously through its loops into a name hard and bright as a spring sky. I let myself stare a moment, then squeak my fingers over the words, swatting dust up into the air, which makes me sneeze, lose balance, and take flight, just as the phone rings. I run downstairs and pick it up in the den.

"Holland? You sound out of breath."

"I was running."

"How's your sister?"

"Better since she got her way."

I imagine Mom on the other end of the line, a silver button earring in one hand while the other cups the mouthpiece. "I can be home by eleven, I think, if Lucy can cover my phone."

"Don't worry about us. When we got home—" Then I stop. If I remind her that Annie is painting here this morning, Mom might send me back to Ambrose. "When we got home," I repeat, more slowly, working out the lie, "Geneva said she felt better, and we're going back to school after lunch."

"Really?"

"She said she wanted to start the day over. She was never that sick, it was mostly a temper tantrum."

Mom exhales through her nose, a sound like wind through leaves. "And you'll call me if the plan changes? Because I really don't want you missing school, Holland."

"Don't worry about us, Mom. I'll take of everything."

"Well, all right." Mom sounds uncertain. "If you're sure. Call if you need me."

"Bye, Mom."

The bad aftertaste of deceit lingers in my mouth after I hang up the phone. I run into the kitchen; maybe a cup of Annie's coffee will smooth it over.

"A couple of things everyone should know about painting a mural," Annie is saying as I join them. She and my sister sit cross-legged on the kitchen floor. Geneva's face is rapt with concentration.

"Sit down," Geneva says, "and listen."

"This is actually a low-intensity bleach, which cleans the walls of any impurities." Annie knocks her hand on a large metal pail beside her. "So don't drink it. There are rags here as well, so today we'll just scrub, scrub,

scrub, then go over the walls with a flat finish, standard undercoat, which is like priming your canvas before you begin your masterpiece. Boring, but it has to be done. These are roller brushes, so it shouldn't take too long.

"Now, since we're going with Geneva's fabulous birds of paradise theme, I'll draw up the final sketches. The sketches are called thumbnails, and they'll be our blueprint. Then we make an outline on the wall using chalk, which is thicker than pencil and erases easily with water if you mess up. Painting is the last step. Since we're doing all our detail in oil, we have to be sure we like the outline, because oil never completely dries, so it's harder to adjust than chalk. Questions?"

Geneva's hand shoots up. "How long will it last?"

"It'll last until you decide to paint over it."

"No, I mean, how long will it take? To paint the kitchen?"

"A couple of weeks, maybe? We won't rush it."

"If we never finish it, then do you stay with us for always?" asks Geneva.

Annie's smile illuminates her face. "Sorry. Like any job, there's a beginning and an end," she says. "Okay, enough talk." She claps her hands. We rise.

"I'll get my radio," Geneva volunteers. She jumps out of the kitchen and hits the stairs running, probably petrified to lose one precious moment with Annie.

"It's like you put her under a spell," I say quietly as I rip one of the old pillowcases Annie tosses me.

"You really care about your sister," she says. "That's important. I don't know anything about having a sister. You girls are so close, I can feel the crackle in the air between you."

"Annie, are you some kind of counselor?" I ask. "Did my dad hire you to help with Geneva?"

"Just a painter. Like I said," Annie answers cheerfully. "I'm here to spruce up this kitchen, give you something new to look at. But you don't have to stay here. Go back to school now, if you like."

"If you don't mind, I think I'll stay. To keep an eye on Geneva."

"Fair enough."

"What's fair enough?" Geneva appears, her portable radio in hand.

"It's fair enough to guess that Holland must have a boyfriend by now, hmm?"

"How'd you know?" Geneva exclaims. "He

litters."

"What's his name?" Annie asks.

"Louis Littlebird."

"He's in ninth grade and he wears a leather jacket like in *Grease*."

"Quiet, Geneva."

"How long have you been seeing him?" Annie asks me.

"I'm not. I saw him wrestle, once. But that wasn't like a date or anything."

"You should invite him over here to help paint. That's not like a date or anything, either."

"No, I don't think so." The idea. How out of touch.

"Mom would despise him," Geneva interjects. "She wouldn't let him come over. He looks like he'd steal things."

"Moms are supposed to dislike boyfriends," says Annie. "The good ones, anyway. It's the law."

"Is that guy, the actor, is he your boyfriend?" Geneva asks.

"We have a relationship," Annie answers with a wink. "But that's between us."

The walls are horribly dirty. We find wash pails under the sink and fill them with warm water and bleach. Then we get to work.

"I adore water," Geneva announces after a

while. She wrings out her rag over the pail and stares into the dingy water. "Especially the sound of waves. Down the shore is my favorite place in the whole wide world."

"Ever seen the beaches in the Caribbean? Now that's gorgeous." Annie sighs. "Romantic."

"No, but we go to Cape May in New Jersey for a couple of weeks every August," I say. "We've only been outside the United States once, to France, when I was eight. Dad won a science award, and we went to the banquet and ceremony and stuff."

"I got food poisoning from a bad periwinkle," Geneva says. "That's all I remember about France."

"There's probably more to France than bad periwinkles," Annie says. "You could go back when you're older."

"Our parents stopped traveling after Geneva was born. Before that, they went all over the world."

"We were named for the places we were conceived in," Geneva adds. "Our Uncle Nelson told us so last time he visited. Remember Holland? How he pointed his cigar at you and said, 'Lucky they decided to baptize you for the country, otherwise we'd be calling you Antwerp, my girl,' and then Mom went,

'Oh, quiet, Nelson, you ridiculous drunk,' and then she grabbed away his wine glass and some spilled on the rug—cigar ash, I mean, not wine—and Uncle Nelson stomped it in, not on purpose, although Mom said it was, secretly."

We laugh together. The parents always had maintained that they named us for places they liked to remember, but until Uncle Nelson's giveaway, we had never understood why our names had been singled out above other favorites, like Paris and India. Now I take new appreciation in my name, knowing that it is so intimate.

"But after a while they stopped traveling," I tell Annie. "It was harder, I guess, with a new family. Now we rarely go anywhere at all."

"Too bad for you. Of course, my friends Dana and Ryan Hubbard vacation every year in Saint Germaine. The good life, hmm?"

"The Hubbards!" I suck in my breath. "How do you know the Hubbards?" The Hubbards are old friends of the parents. They have rented our bungalow in Saint Germaine since before I can remember. The parents never sold the bungalow—once I heard Mom tell Brett and Carla that renting is a better investment, but I am sure there are other, more intricate reasons for their holding onto that property.

The Hubbards are nothing more to me than their blandly smiling faces in some slides and photographs, an entry in Dad's address book, and the occasional letter that arrives in the mail and contains a few boring paragraphs comparing the weather in Saint Germaine with Seattle's.

The notes always end with a P.S. request that Geneva and I come visit them in either place, but the parents tell us they're just being polite—who would really want to look after two young girls, especially during their holiday? So I have never met the Hubbards, and they remain part of another life, built into the dark and secret passages of a different family's history.

"I've known the Hubbards forever," Annie says. "I painted a mural for them in the pantry of their house down in Saint Germaine. An elm tree."

"Their pantry? You mean our pantry—it's our house—they rent it from us!" I turn to my sister. "That's so strange, don't you think so, Geneva? I mean, here she's been to Saint Germaine, and met the Hubbards even, and we didn't know."

"I always wanted to see Saint Germaine!" Geneva bursts out. "It looks so adorable in the pictures. We've never been to Seattle, either, not that I really want to go there, I hear there's lots of traffic jams. But I especially want to visit Saint Germaine, more than the shore. More than anywhere."

"Be quiet, stupid. We can never go there."

"You be quiet, you said so your stupid self that you wanted to visit." She looks at Annie. "They all used to visit every year, sometimes twice a year. Mom and Dad said it's the most beautiful place on earth. There's tons of slides and pictures of them, on the fishing boat, or at Starling Cove, or—"

"The parents would never take us there! There are a million places to go instead of there!"

"Don't shout at me, Holland, I'm right here next to you!" Geneva shouts. "And you don't need to try and make me feel bad when I know you want to see it, too, okay? Just because something happened there seven years before I was even born doesn't mean I can't wonder what Saint Germaine's like, especially since I've seen all those pictures of it, and even Brett and Carla stayed at the house last year, and—"

"Time out." Annie makes a referee's signal. "Listen, I wouldn't have brought up Saint Germaine at all if I knew it meant witnessing this shouting match. Let's get back to work. Holland, since you're taller, would you wipe over the parts of the wall Geneva can't reach? Cooperation counts on this project."

"Sorry, Holland. I didn't mean to shout," Geneva mutters, which is so uncharacteristic that I say sorry back.

"What are they like?" I ask after a few minutes.

"Who?"

"The *Hubbards*, Annie. Are they nice?"

"Oh, you should meet them, they're a pair," Annie says. "I bet they would love to meet you."

"The parents wouldn't let us," Geneva says through gritted teeth. "They have their own way of doing things, which mostly means doing nothing."

I give up on the conversation and attack the wall with my rag. The radio moans through one cozy love song after another. I imagine Louis Littlebird standing under the arches of Washington Square Park. He holds a bunch of daisies behind his back and offers them to me as I swing up to greet him, just like in that deodorant commercial. I press my nose into his neck and my cheek brushes the leather of his jacket; my laugh is an unfamiliar, throaty gurgle that I'm sure I could perfect in real life. In my fantasies, I am as Ick as I want to be.

"I'm starving," Geneva says, breaking into my daydreams.

"Didn't you pack lunch?" Annie asks. "Eat that." Geneva frowns; it was not the answer she had hoped for. Annie cooking up omelettes, Annie springing for lunch at Les Deux Gamins—I am sure this is what Geneva wanted. But we unwrap our brown bag lunches without argument and eat our cheese sandwiches, grapes, and shortbread cookies. Geneva talks with her mouth full, firing questions at Annie as she continues to clean the walls.

"How much are you getting paid?" Geneva asks.

"Enough," Annie answers. "Standard rate."

"Is art your full-time job?"

"You could say that."

"Where do you live?"

"Uptown."

"How high? Seventies, Eighties, Nineties?"

She jabs her thumb northward. "A little higher." Geneva and I share a look; we have never heard of anyone living higher than Professor Nolan, a friend of Dad's who lives on 121st Street. Then Geneva resumes her silly questions.

"Are you and Jack married?"

"No."

"Have you talked about getting married?"

"You know, I don't think about it."

"Do you miss him, like right now do you?"

Annie pauses in her work. "Not so much, because I always feel like I'm with him, even when I'm not."

After lunch, we start priming. Annie is tireless, spinning on the toes of her ugly shoes as she directs our brush strokes. Priming the walls with our base coat takes up most of the early afternoon. After we are finished I am exhausted, ready to lounge in the den with a cool drink in one hand and the remote control in the other.

"So," Annie says as she stands in the middle of the kitchen, hands on her hips, surveying our work, "who's ready for a downtown adventure? We have time." She pops the paint-thickened roller from its handle and wraps it in newspaper before dropping it in the trash.

"Adventure, adventure!" Geneva executes a poorly skilled Irish step dance around the kitchen. "Let's go!"

"I don't know." I hold my breath, indecisive. "People might report us, since we should be in school."

"This is New York," Annie says. "People are too busy with their own lives to care about yours. Of course, anybody who wants to stay home or go back to school is certainly allowed."

Geneva needs no coaxing. I decide I have to follow, if only to baby-sit.

mr. depass and miss pia

The E train carries a handful of weary passengers who stare at us as we slide into the plastic seats. A few senior citizens, a man eating from a bag of rust-colored chips, and a couple with matching purple Kool-Aid dyed hair and silver rings stuck in their bellybuttons all stare a moment and then dismiss us. I wonder how I appear to strangers: a prissy Catholic-school girl wearing a boiled wool jacket (I couldn't find my windbreaker) and jeans.

"We'll get off at Spring Street," Annie says. "Decent shopping there."

"Shopping?" Geneva asks. Her hands are packaged neatly on her lap. She hadn't planned on taking the subway; nor had I, but it's easier for me to adjust to the unexpected than it is for my sister. She looks as if she might be sick. To Geneva, a subway is a filthy, hissing, germ-infested beast far more dangerous than his brother—the barely domesticated but tolerable taxicab. Annie's insistence that subways are quicker was the last word over Geneva's protest. Now she chews her lip and tightens herself into the smallest amount of space that her body will permit.

The advertisements pasted to the subway walls are the wallpaper of a world more edgy than the manicured lap dogs and chicken-wire-ringed shrubbery of our neighborhood. HANDS ARE MEANT FOR HOLDING bellows the type block across one poster, showing a black-and-white photograph of a knuckle-clubbed fist. Phone numbers and addresses of local battered women's shelters are printed in large type below the fist. Another poster advises people to get regular checkups for the diseases they might or might not have. Still another bulletin lectures on the dangers of needle-sharing. Geneva's eyes are buggy, staring at the forlorn faces of poster board junkies.

"I hate this subway," she whispers. "I need to wash my hands."

"Nowhere to wash on the subway. You'll have to suck it up and wait till we get off," Annie answers. We both look at her, startled. Did Annie actually hear the secret voice?

"How much longer?" Geneva asks in the same pitch, testing Annie.

"More soon than later," Annie answers, and she opens her face into a giant kidlike yawn, to prove how disinterested she is in Geneva's needs.

Geneva tucks her hands in her armpits and whispers Hail Marys until the subway stops at Spring Street.

Soho is packed with its usual mix of self-consciously fashionable locals and frowzy tourists. The smell of roasted peanuts and spicy falafels wafts from the street vendors' grills and drifts through the air.

"Let's hit the vintage stores," Annie says after we stop at a diner and wait while Geneva runs into the rest room. Soho has sent a jolt of exhilaration through Annie. As soon as Geneva emerges, Annie breaks into a stride down the street, and it becomes impossible for Geneva and me to keep pace without taking a few jogging steps every half block. Annie holds her chin up and keeps her hands pushed inside her blazer pockets. It is a deliberate gesture; she does not want to hold our hands. Annie does not touch, I have noticed. It might be one of the reasons Geneva has been so quick to adore her.

"Good shops are hard to find since this part of town's so commercial lately. The true clotheshound will prevail. I remember once when I was about your age, Holland, I wore a tutu to a Valentine's Day dance, a semiformal. I found it in a store called the Basement Boutique, but the tulle had gone ratty. So I bought a length of dark blue chenille at one of the fabric shops in Alphabet City, and I recovered the whole dress. Tulle is like a canvas, a base coat. Chenille, on the other hand, sets a mood."

"Did you wear ballet shoes, too?" Geneva asks breathlessly.

"Tap shoes, actually, with the taps still in," Annie answers. "I made the most noise on the dance floor, even if I didn't have the best moves. Jack wore a painted tuxedo T-shirt. I guess that sounds awful now, but we thought we were stunning. Here it is." She stops at the corner of a brick-bunkered side street. We stare at the outside of a glass door so filthy I cannot see in.

"Five-Star Vintage Clothing and Consignment," I read the words scrolled on the shop's torn awning. "In a class by itself."

"Hello!" Annie calls as we step inside the shop. "Mr. DePass?"

A man behind the counter does not look up from his newspaper. He wears his graying hair loose over his shoulders and his checker-and-rhinestone shirt gives him the look of some kind of cowboy poet.

"Mr. DePass!" Annie exclaims. She tucks her arms in front of her chest, surveying him. Her feet in their strappy shoes rock back and forth.

Mr. DePass eventually glances up at us. I catch a twinkle of his bejeweled fingers as he flips them through his hair. "Yeah?" He peers forward and looks at us.

"I haven't been here in so long," Annie says apologetically. "But it smells exactly the same." I sniff the air politely and inhale a faint scent of carbon paper and feet.

"We're just going to look around," I say to Mr. DePass.

"Feel free," he answers, focusing back on his paper.

"Something's changed," Annie says, moving into the crowded heart of the store. "Is the lower level where the on-sale clothes are?" She runs her hands along the racks of soft fabrics.

"Does the lower level have sales?" I raise my voice. Poor old Mr. DePass seems to be going deaf. He looks up, startled, and shakes his head.

"Sales in back. The basement's my music studio now," he answers. He points to me, and I notice that, in addition to his assortment of rings, he wears black fingernail polish. "You." He smiles at me, flashing a jumbled row of teeth. "I know you from somewhere, sometime a while back, right?"

"I don't think so." I pretend to ponder his features, although I am certain that I have never seen the man before in my life.

"Come look at this, guys." Annie's voice calls out from the back of the store. Mr. DePass nods.

"Might be I'm wrong. Probably seen one too many faces come through my shop." He dismisses me with a wave. "Go on, have a look in back. I just got a pile of loot from the East End Theater Company that'll interest you."

Geneva and I find Annie surveying a mountain of clothing piled on a folding chair. "This place is still as big a mess as ever," she says happily. "I never get back here anymore, since I moved. Look—spectacular." She points to a royal blue jacket trimmed with gold braid. "Try it on."

"Me?" I am already shedding my wool coat to slide one arm, then the next, through the blue-and-gold-striped satin lining. "It's loose."

The mottled mirror reflects a girl lost deep inside a pageant style blazer. The longer I look, though, the more I see myself in the coat, and the more the coat becomes me. "I'm sure I don't have enough money," I say.

"Bet you could swap it," Annie says. "For the one you walked in with." I hear Geneva's delighted intake of breath at the nerve of the suggestion.

"Mom would be angry," I say. "That is, even if Mr. DePass wants my Ambrose coat to begin with."

"Holland, hand it over. Geneva, go check." I toss my wool jacket to Geneva, who trots to the front of the store.

"I'm making her an accomplice," I say.

"What's the use of having a sister if she can't be an accomplice?"

"Holland," Geneva calls. "He says come up here so he can make sure we're talking about the same jacket."

Mr. DePass's ornamented fingers are rubbing the sleeve of my jacket as we approach. "It's a decent quality wool here," he says. "There's enough to take down the cuffs, too. I got a customer, he does an Audrey Hepburn act down at the Chateau Hip, I bet he'd pay some good money for this. It's a trade, if you want to walk out in what you got on."

"Deal," I say before my logical mind can stop me. I feel the compulsive twinge of a gambler about to play a crucial stack of chips. Not only will Mom be furious, not only am I setting a bad example for my little sister, but somehow I feel that I have succumbed to the temptation of Annie, and I have become her accomplice just as Geneva has become mine.

When I walk back into daylight I feel altered, and I do not know which is the braver act, wearing my new jacket or leaving my old one behind.

"You look cool," Geneva says. "I saw a hat in there I liked. Maybe this weekend we can come down here and get it."

"It's far to walk."

"We could take the subway," she says. "It's easier to take a subway to a place you want to go than to somewhere boring. I like Soho. Annie's right, no one pays attention to us. Ooh, look at that place—'Miss Pia's Psychic Readings and

Advice.'" Geneva points across the street to a ground-level storefront. "I have money. I want a fortune."

"Go get one then," Annie says. "But hurry. I can't hang out all day." When I look over at Annie, I notice that her hair is clumping around her shoulders and that her face and neck glow in the rich afternoon sunlight.

"I know that shop," she says.

"It's probably a ripoff."

"Only for skeptics," Annie says in such a way that I can't tell if she herself is a skeptic or not.

We watch Geneva cross the street and slide through the door of the fortune teller's shop. She reappears inside the glass picture window, now speaking with Miss Pia, a plump psychic who wears her hair in two braids.

Geneva places some bills on the table between them, then seats herself in the curve-backed chair opposite Miss Pia.

Annie watches, then strides across the street, paying no mind to the charging traffic. A cab driver honks and curses as I rush after her, and I raise my hand in meek apology. Despite her confident stories, I doubt that Annie was the most protective baby-sitter in the city.

"I'm going on a trip," Geneva announces,

not turning around as we duck through the sateen curtains and into the psychic's lair.

"It's late and Annie wants to go," I whisper. A psychic is the last thing Geneva needs— someone to help her troll for nightmares and attach meaning to her ghostly visions. I only hope my sister doesn't bring up her sightings of the mayor.

"Shhh." The woman puts her finger to her lips and regards me haughtily. "You're creating negative energy."

"Sorry," I say, taking a step back. I look over at Annie, who stands in the curtained shadows and stares down at her watch, tapping its face.

"Your sister's a doubter," Miss Pia tattles on me to Geneva. "Remove yourself from this skepticalness so I can see your inner light clearer." The back of Geneva's head moves slightly, realigning herself outside the beam of my negative energy.

Miss Pia leans forward to clutch Geneva's palm, but germ-phobic Geneva snatches it away.

"Can you read without holding?" she asks.

Miss Pia pauses a moment, then recovers and nods. She drops her head, so close her eyelashes could kiss Geneva's fingers. "Like I said, you are going on a journey," she intones in a phony dramatic cadence. "You have been confused for a real long time. Which is from a problem. This problem is hard to see. I do not know where your journey takes you. Aha but wait. A man or a lady appears in your future. He maybe she holds three roses. One rose is for beauty. One is for chance. The last rose—"

"She's allergic to roses," I grumble. Annie hiccups a laugh.

"Come on!" Geneva exclaims, twisting in her chair to frown at us.

"Who's there?" the psychic asks, looking past Geneva.

"Oh, they're with me," Geneva answers. "Go on, back to the fortune. What is the last rose for?"

"Who're you?" Miss Pia points at me.

I look at Annie, who shrugs.

"I'm Holland. Holland Shepard."

"Get outta here!" The Dracula accent is gone, replaced by one more distinctly New York in origin. "Shepard, I knew it." She taps her chest. "Pia Kredneck—I went to Ambrose. I was a senior Liz's freshman year. We played on the tennis team together. She was excellent at tennis. I knew Johnnie Shepard better—same grade. Even went on a double date with him. He wasn't my date, though, he went out with Suki Miller, but I went out with his best buddy,

Lentil—Len Tillman—which is how I met Johnnie."

I nod. I know Suki Miller, John's high school girlfriend, who is now Suki Miller Slatey. Mom always says Suki would have been her daughter-in-law, and last year on John's birthday Suki even sent us some hand-marbleized coasters and such a long letter about missing John that Mom suspected that Suki's marriage might be heading for trouble. Lentil keeps in touch, too. He's been living in Seattle and is the father of five-year-old twins. He sent us a cute picture of their last birth-day party, two dark-haired boys covered in white frosting. The picture is somewhere in the house, tucked into a drawer with the marbleized coasters and other like mementos.

"I saw you in the door, and I kept thinking, Who does she remind me of? You could be Liz, I swear!" Pia stands, hands on her hips, Geneva's fortune forgotten. "Get over here, let me take a look!"

She reaches across the table and pumps my hand, and her robe falls open to reveal a pair of spandex jogging pants and a halter top.

"Wow, so this is so something, so surrealish. A long time ago now, but still, looking at you brings me back. Jeez."

"And this is my sister, Geneva," I mention. Pia registers the introduction with a faint wave in Geneva's direction; her thoughts are focused elsewhere.

"That memorial service was, I mean, you couldn't even get in the churchyard. I was there, I wouldn't have missed it, paying respects. Three kids in one family, it was like you couldn't stop thinking about it, talking about it. In college I heard you were born, and I was so psyched for your parents. Seemed real positive, after all that negative. I sent over a pair of pink sparkle booties." She smiles, spacing a finger and thumb an inch apart. "Teeny little baby shoes, pink hearts on the toes."

"I don't really remember them," I say awkwardly. "But, um, thanks. Oh, I should— this is Annie." I turn, but Annie is gone.

"Hey." Geneva stands up. "Where'd she go?" She skirts past me, out the door and into the street, leaving me to indulge Pia Kredneck's memories.

And talk Pia does, many of the same stories that I have heard before, from Brett—how John loved Pink Floyd and followed their concerts up and down the coast, and the time he made bird noises over the school intercom. Then she tells me a new story about Elizabeth being one of the only freshman allowed to sit in the senior lounge because she played varsity tennis. Once

Pia gets going on high school memories, she can't stop, and I nod and listen and think about Geneva turned loose on the streets of Soho. I am relieved when Pia says she has a date tonight and wants to close shop early.

"I'll come back and visit," I promise. "It's always great to meet people who knew my brothers and sister." The parents can be selective about who they invite into our home, and to look at Pia is to know she did not make the cut, which is a shame because she seems very lively. Plus you could get all those free lessons on how to read tea leaves and palms.

"Oh, yeah." Pia's little braids quiver as she nods. "Totally. I live upstairs. We'll put on some Floyd, dish up the old times."

After they get a little tipsy on the memories, people who knew my old family almost inevitably forget that I never did.

I help her lock up—two glass doors, then a roll-down metal grill—and after she is gone I sit on her stoop and wait. I catch sight of my reflection in the restaurant window across the street. The gold buttons of my jacket flash like gentle stars in their blue sky of fabric. I shift my hand to watch the change in my reflection, to make sure I am really here.

"There you are!"

"Annie said she'd see us later." Geneva has crept up to my side, puffing short breaths. "She walks too quick. I didn't feel like following."

"We better get home."

She squints at Miss Pia's shop. "Where'd she go? What about my fortune?"

"Next time. It's almost six, anyway." I pat the pockets of my coat and realize that the few bills I brought with me are back at the thrift shop, tucked in a pocket of my old wool jacket. "Do you have any money?"

Geneva shakes her head. "I spent it on Miss Pia."

"Figures."

"But she said I was going on a trip. What do you think she meant by that?"

"She wanted to make you happy so you felt like it was worth your money. There's no such thing as a real fortune teller." I grip Geneva's fingers in my hand. "There's no such thing as a psychic, or a future predictor, or whatever you want to call it. It's not real."

"I always thought that what makes some-thing real is deciding it is." Geneva readjusts her hand so that it notches more tightly into mine. "I wish I knew what that last rose was for, though," she says sadly, with a small backward glance at the shop.

"Who cares?" I say. "You make your own fortune, right?"

And yet it seems sort of typical that the story of my sister's future was interrupted in order to tell the tales of my family's past.

louis and seven mom

"That's a cool jacket. Military style." Louis salutes me and smiles.

"She traded it for her other one at a thrift shop yesterday. This morning she sneaked it out of the house in her book bag." For once, Geneva makes me look better instead of worse. Louis whistles approvingly.

We have bumped into each other in front of our vendor again this morning. Louis knew I would be here. I could tell by the way he stood, looking down the block when Geneva and I were no more than two specks drifting up the sidewalk. I knew by the way that he dawdled, drinking his juice, that he was waiting *for me*. The thought is still spiking my stomach as my mind memorizes images to savor later. Louis Littlebird has a chip in his bottom front tooth. Louis Littlebird wears a silver chain around his neck and a plain gray sweatshirt under his leather jacket today.

"I'll walk you two over to Ambrose, if you want," Louis says. "I got time."

Geneva pushes ahead of us. "I can escort myself," she declares over her shoulder. I could give her a hug right then for good sisterliness. I did not even have to make a bet.

Louis walks with a fighting lift in his jaw and a sleepy smile that makes him appear relaxed and thoughtful. I want to imitate his style, to take something of his and make it my own.

"So where do you usually hang out after school?" he asks. "You and your friends."

"Oh, you know. Chatterbox Diner, for one." Which is not a complete lie. Kathlyn LeDuc and I have been to the Chatterbox on Friday afternoons whenever I stay over at her house, but it is usually my responsibility to bring Geneva home directly after school. But Louis does not need to know that I spend most afternoons taking care of my little sister. "Except this past week, Geneva and I have been heading straight home after school, since we've been helping an artist friend of ours paint our kitchen."

"Sounds boring."

"No, it isn't. Really. We get to paint pictures on the wall."

"Oh, like a mural? My older brother did that once on one of the outside walls of our school. It was a tribute to the Grateful Dead after Jerry Garcia died. He got suspended. But he said some things are more important than rules."

"Totally." I cannot wait to record this story in my L.L. Notebook of Facts.

We turn the corner and he slips his hand into mine. "Know how to thumb wrestle?" he asks. "I'm the undefeated champion in my family. It's easy. Hold your hand in mine like this, all fingers in, but keep your thumb free, like that. Okay, when I say go, try to pin my thumb under yours. Ready?"

"No, wait." I stop walking. "I can't do this and walk. Now I'm ready."

"One two three, go!"

Our thumbs jab and pounce with the mechanized movements of two monsters in an old

Godzilla movie. Louis wins promptly, his thumb squeezing mine bloodless.

"Best outta three," he says, and beats me again.

"Strong thumbs," I comment, shoving my tingling hands in my pockets before he tries for a rematch. "I like that in a guy." I had only meant to make a joke, but I wonder if my comment was too slinky. Thankfully, Louis doesn't seem to mind or notice.

"It's from giving my mom neck rubs. She gets bad headaches. I know all the right pressure points."

Louis's comment seems kind of slinky, too, and I am not sure what to answer, so I do not say anything.

We walk quickly to catch up with Geneva. Words that have been stumbling around in my brain now slip past my lips.

"You could come over," I say. "After school, I mean. To see our mural." I feel the tips of my ears ignite.

"Yeah?"

"I mean, only if you have time."

"As long as I can catch an F train near your house. I'd need to be home by six to help make dinner, otherwise my mom'll holler."

"We're 176 Waverly. Between Greenwich

and Seventh Avenue South, on the corner below West Tenth."

"Yeah, that's easy. Okay. Like four-thirty?"

"Sure. We'll be there. You can meet Annie. She's the artist. She's very cool."

"And your folks?"

"They'll be at work. They won't be home until after six."

"You got food?"

"I think so. Definitely."

"And I can paint, too?"

"Totally."

"Okay. See you there, Sergeant Shepard." Louis salutes me again, then glides to a stop not too short of the curious crowd milling around the school's entryway. Just as I hope, the whispers and stares begin.

"Who was that?" Kathlyn pokes me in the shoulder after Louis moves out of earshot.

"That's Louis Litterbug, Holland's new boyfriend," explains Geneva. "Mom hasn't met him. She'll haaate him," she sings as she skips away to the door where her class is lining up.

"Don't call him that," I call out to her retreating back.

"Quite the leather-clad rebel escort," says Tyra Sharp, a stylish, not altogether friendly girl in my class who gets most of her attitude from the fact that her mom is a made-for-TV movie producer. "Do tell more."

"Do tell," parrots Tyra's best friend, Mindy Bruner. Suddenly I am the focus of more attention than I can remember since I won the tennis award. Except this kind of attention is way better.

"He's coming over this afternoon," I say. From all around me, there are sounds of approval.

Classes seem to double or triple in length as I wait for the day to be over. Louis is my secret to savor and hoard, and I safeguard it with a bet. *If everything goes right with Louis today, then you one-hundred-percent absolutely have to tell the parents about him within the next week.* It will be a hard promise to keep, because I am sure the parents won't like Louis, but I feel better knowing the deal has been made.

"He's coming to our house?" Geneva repeats as we walk home from school that afternoon. "Does Mom know?"

"No, but Annie will be there. She's our supervisor, and she told me to invite him, remember?"

"Sure I remember," Geneva answers.

At home, however, Annie is nowhere to be

found. Books are scattered on the kitchen table, and a box of chalk lies opened on the counter. A thumbnail sketch is taped to the refrigerator.

"Where do you think she went?" Geneva looks depressed. She rolls a stick of chalk over her palm. "Looks like she has everything all set up for us, like she wants us to get started. That must be the final sketch."

"And Louis is coming." A point of fact that seems more hazardous now that Annie's not around. "What are we supposed to do?"

"Change clothes, first off. You don't want him to think you wear your dumb uniform out of school. And you have pen on your cheek."

"Oh, gross!" There is no time to think in the next fifteen minutes, as I concentrate on unearthing the right T-shirt to go with my jeans, brushing my hair fifty flattening strokes, borrowing one of Mom's hair combs—then tossing it back on her dresser when the hair style makes me look like I tried too hard—and going through the business of sketching on and wiping off makeup.

I do not even hear the rattle of the front gate, or the doorbell.

"He's here!" yells Geneva.

I squint one last time in my bedroom mirror, then the hall mirror, rub off more lipstick with the back of my hand, and glide down the stairs.

Geneva and Louis are standing in the kitchen. "It's called a *trompe l'oeil*," Geneva is explaining in her know-it-all voice, "which means trick of the eye in French. That's what we and Annie are making in our kitchen." She grabs one of the opened books on the table. "See? These birds are my idea. It's going to be like a tropical paradise, sky all around. Cerulean blue plus cadmium scarlet are my bird colors. I picked them out."

"I never saw anyone's kitchen look like paradise," Louis says with a smile as he glances over at me. I wave.

"We have creamsicles and salt-and-vinegar potato chips," I tell him. I had practiced saying this sentence in the mirror and it comes out perfectly.

"What's wrong with your voice, Holland?" asks Geneva. "If you're getting a cold, don't come near me. I'm very susceptible," she informs Louis.

"Aren't we all," Louis replies seriously. "Do you have juice?"

"Yep." I move to the fridge and cupboard.

"And we have coffee. Look, Holland, did you notice Annie left a full pot on?"

"Oh, great." It is Annie's own blend, too. Inhaling the warmth of spicy vanilla nutmeg makes me feel more at ease. "The artist came by earlier to set up," I explain to Louis. "But who knows where she is now. She's a little bit random." I hand Louis a glass of orange juice, which he drains in an instant and hands back for a refill. His fingertips graze mine in the exchange; they are rough as bark, warm as summer. The sensation leaves me dizzy.

"She from around here?" Louis asks. He picks up a piece of chalk and jiggles a blue line on the wall, then steps back to look at it.

"She lives uptown," I explain, "but she's an artsy type. Her boyfriend's an actor." I immediately wish I hadn't said the word boyfriend, since Louis might think that I consider him to be my boyfriend, or am considering boyfriends in general. He doesn't seem to notice.

"I can do those trees," Louis says, pointing to the refrigerator. "The sketch shows that you're going to put a big spiky one right here. I'll do that one, if you want."

"I'm like the worst artist in my class, so if I'm allowed to paint, you definitely can."

"She's great at science," Geneva says. "You should see her cell diorama. She got a ribbon."

"Whoa," says Louis. I can't tell if he's being

sarcastic or not, so I just roll my eyes and say nothing.

Geneva turns on the radio and Louis changes the dial.

"University station," he explains. "It plays all the buzz clips, no repeats."

"I never knew the University had its own music station," I say.

"Our dad works for the University," Geneva tells Louis.

"If your own dad works for the University, how could you two not know about this station?" he asks.

"He's kind of old," I admit.

"*I* knew about it," Geneva says unconvincingly.

Louis uses bold, decisive outlines to define his sketch, so that the shape of his tree becomes as strong as the shape of the space around it. Geneva concentrates on details. She works on a far corner of the kitchen, filling a bird of paradise into the arm of a free-floating branch. The bird's plumed head and rubbery toes are in perfect proportion. The leaves of my own sad shrub are a blur of uncertainty: nothing like the "espalier" diagram I am trying to copy from one of Annie's books. No matter how I move my chalk against the wall, I cannot give life to my plant.

"I want my kneaded eraser," I grumble after a while. Louis and Geneva barely acknowledge my words. Their chalkings are gorgeous compared with my own smudges. As I'm leaving the kitchen, I allow myself a glance at the lazy ripple of muscle that moves across Louis's back as he works. He wears his sweatpants low, and I can see the white band of his underwear elastic. I watch for a while.

Upstairs, I cannot locate my eraser. I kneel on the floor and quickly dump out the top drawer of my desk. I don't even know what I am doing up here, or why I care so much about finding the stupid eraser, anyway. It won't make my sketch better, that's for sure. A hot sweat begins to stick under my arms. I should change my T-shirt. No, that would look like I'm thinking about my outfits too much. I stand up and grab my deodorant, then bang it down again. I feel desperate.

Something about Louis's presence in the kitchen makes me want to run. I imagine a panting flight out the front door, up the street to the Peacock Caffé, where I can sip an Italian soda in solitude. But running is not an option, not now.

Again I drop to crouch over the spilled contents of my desk. Still no eraser. I stand up and fling open the drawers of my dresser, recklessly searching for a T-shirt. In the half hour that he has been in my home, I could fill my entire notebook with facts about Louis Littlebird. The problem is that this Louis is more unpredictable than his notebook entries. He cannot be closed up inside a desk and savored between classes. Just thinking about writing in my notebook conjures up an image of my sweaty handprints, damp over the pages and plastic cover, and I realize my notebook, and my invented Louis, are no good to me anymore. The real Louis will not bend in the directions I choose, or beam back the thoughts that I project like light into a mirror.

Imaginary people are so much easier.

Fingers tap at the door.

"Yes?"

"It's me."

"You can come in."

"Hey." Louis stands in my room, an alien in my oasis of girlishness. His gaze skims my matching furniture, and I want to hide a dozen things—my horse posters and my Madame Alexander doll collection, to start. "Find your eraser?"

"I'm still looking."

"Your sister's like, *intense* about that bird. I don't even think she noticed I left the kitchen to find you. Anyhow, I quit art for today. Come downstairs and admire my tree."

"Okay."

But instead of going downstairs, Louis ambles past me to the edge of my bed, where he sits and then stretches out on his back, lying halfway across the bedspread while his feet remain planted on the floor. I wonder if my bed will smell like Louis after he gets up. A thrilling thought. "I'm beat," he says. "Tryouts killed me. I hope I make JV."

I move to the end of my bed and lean the tops of my legs against it, hugging my arms across my chest. The position looks and feels awkward. I cannot think of a word to say to him; I am just so elated and horrified that he is here in my room.

"Got any pets?" Louis asks.

"No. Our parents say we're the pets," I retell their joke lamely.

"Not even a pigeon or a rat? A cute New York City pet?"

"They think pets are messy."

"They're right—animals can destroy a house. You have a nice place, a nice room." Louis turns to me, yawning. His hair flops over his eyes, and I think of Shetland ponies, gypsies, rock stars. "Our house is like Noah's ark.

Besides having two dogs, an eleven-year-old cat, and a pair of guinea pigs who we hoped were both boys—but now one looks pregnant—I got two older sisters and one older brother. Then there's me, and I share a room with Matthew, Mattie, we call him. The youngest. Five kids, total."

"Do you like being a big brother?"

"Mattie's two years younger than your sister and two times the problem."

"How's that?"

"I witnessed her in action," Louis says, "and I never saw her bite. Which is what Mattie's up to these days. As soon as you tell him he should get ready for bed or finish his veggies—chomp! Right in the arm. Like this."

Louis opens his mouth wide and grabs my hand. I watch his teeth sink into the skin of my wrist.

"Stop." I pull my hand away, because I like it too much. Louis grins. He opens his mouth wide and snaps at the air like a crocodile.

"Hey, you don't have any cavities," I say.

"Yeah-huh. I got two." Louis opens his mouth and jams his finger somewhere deep in back of his mouth. "Ahh? Ah ga oo, heyaa!"

I duck my head. "Eww, I don't want to see—" I stop speaking when I feel Louis's hand encircle my wrist again. "What?" I ask. I feel my mouth smiling although I do not feel smiley, exactly, because all my nerves are curled like electric wires inside me. "What?" I ask again as he uses his grip on me as a leverage to pull himself up from the bed, and then we are facing each other, too close to talk, too close to breathe, and Louis bends his head so there is no more height between us, and I move one way and he moves another way, and then I tip my mouth up to meet his mouth and our lips touch, almost, and I feel his breath, smelling faintly of orange juice, but warm and good.

I give in to the sensation of Louis, and my fingers move cautiously over his shoulders, up and up to touch the warm, alive pulse of his neck. Its rhythm pushes against my fingertips like the code of a secret language.

I lift myself onto my tiptoes, and then I feel his mouth for real this time. His arm is as thick as a branch of tree for me to lean against, and his sweatshirt smells like dust and skin and—

"Oh, Holland, no!"

For the second time this afternoon, I did not hear the door. Her voice is more clipped than angry, but the sound rockets me off, away, streaming away from Louis. When I recollect myself my back is pressed up hard against my dresser; its brass handles are pinching my skin, and my face is pepper red and hot, and my eyes sting at the sound of her dismay.

Mom.

vincent and aaron

Everyone is asleep. My watch reads one minute to one in the morning. I sit in Elizabeth's desk chair. By the soft streetlight, I can see well enough to scratch my fingernail over the initials in Elizabeth's desk. E. S. + W. J.

Did W. J. ever sneak a visit to 176 Waverly? Did Mom ever catch Elizabeth kissing W. J., or any guy, in this same room and cry, "Oh, Elizabeth, no!" Did Elizabeth ever think about spending her whole allowance on a one-way bus ticket to Orlando, Florida, to get away from this house of silent disapproval?

The entire afternoon had collapsed in ruins within a few earthquaking seconds. Mom ordered Louis out of the house immediately, saying she did not "even want to know your name, young man." Louis had gone quietly, making the sign of a telephone receiver with one hand, the other pointing to me, then cheerfully waving good-bye as if the situation were more of a bother than a total humiliation.

Mom immediately demanded an explanation that she had practically no interest in hearing, because every time I tried to tell her about Geneva, or Louis, or Annie, she interrupted by saying how disappointed she was in me and what a bad example I set for Geneva and what kind of school was Ambrose, anyway, if it couldn't teach her daughter decent Christian behavior.

Later, at dinner, she and Dad decided to ground me, the first formal punishment dealt out to me since second grade, when I ran away from home and got as far as Christopher Park. Dad had discovered me less than half an hour later, sitting on a bench and holding a lunch box packed full of clean underwear and plastic forks. I was grounded then (for a day), and I have been grounded now (starting tomorrow, Friday, all the way through to next Sunday).

The very worst moment of the entire

evening, however, occurred just a few hours ago, at bedtime, when Mom again walked into my room unannounced.

"Good night, Holland," she said, setting a crinkly puckered kiss on my forehead. "I hope when you stop crying, you might use this day as a learning experience."

"Mmm-hmm."

"And I hope you think your punishment is fair and not too strict. We hate to punish, your dad and I."

"Mmm-hmm."

She sighed. "I also wanted to talk to you about something else," she began. "That boy you were with. He's an older boy."

"Ninth grade at Bishop Brown, same as Aaron Hill. One stupid year older than me."

"You don't need to be so surly, Holland. All I mean to say is . . ." Mom drew a breath and tried again. "Boys like that, who look older, they're usually wild, troublesome. They want attention. They want . . . things, and I'm not speaking rashly, but someone like Aaron Hill—not that it would have to be Aaron, except that you've known him all your life—but someone like Aaron, just might be exactly the kind of boyfriend you can grow into." She laughed. "For lack of a better phrase."

"Mom, a guy is not like something sold at Macy's, for you to pick out and pay for and bring home to me. Secondly, for your information, Aaron Hill is in the same grade as Louis. And you know what?" My voice was sliding up precariously high scales, but I could not stop. "Louis told me the entire ninth grade at Bishop Brown calls him Aaron the Pious as a joke because he's so up on himself, so there!"

"How hateful of you, Holland. What a poisonous thing to say." Mom seemed to fold into herself as she adjusted her bathrobe belt tighter across her front. "I hope when you're feeling more rational the two of us can sit down and have a mature conversation." She turned and began to walk out of the room.

"Were the buggies ever bad?" A biting hook of a question, and when she faced me again I was suddenly, vindictively glad for the ache behind her eyes. I know all the other Shepards' now unmentionable nicknames from old letters and yearbooks and Christmas cards: John-boy, Johnnie, Dizzy, Lizbit, K. P. (for Kevin Paul). But this name, goofy and alien in my mouth, was Mom's Ick name for all of them. "Three snugbuggies," she had written on the back of a stray photograph showing them all wrapped in winter coats and mufflers, and once I found an old letter to Mom from Dana Hubbard with a P.S. sending "all the love in the world to your buggies."

"Do you enjoy hurting me, Holland?" Mom asked, words that almost paralyzed me with guilt and rage.

"Were they?" I demanded, red-faced and stubborn, hating myself, as she walked out of my room and closed the door behind her. Because Kevin joined a fraternity, I wanted to shout, and I know enough about fraternities from kids at school whose older brothers pledged and pinned. Fraternities are all about drinking and girls, dirty jokes and broken rules. And John must have been in some trouble for doing those bird noises on the school intercom.

Now, at one to one in the morning, the question again surfaces in my thoughts. Did the other Shepards ever disobey? Did Elizabeth only date nice boys? I never heard of a boy with the initials W. J. Then again, I never heard of Pia Kredneck. I probably never heard of a lot of things that happened here over two decades ago.

The problem with living in a house full of angels is that each year they soar just a little bit higher, and their memories turn into brokenhearted carols sung only to praise their time on earth. Fraternity pranks and missed curfews are forgotten, inadequate boyfriends are forgotten; after eighteen years all the parents want to hear are the hymns and the peaceful rustle of distant wings, while my sister and I remain weighted by the burden of our own unhaloed heads.

I try to picture W. J. lurking in the shadows, wearing a leather jacket and chewing a tooth-pick. Then I picture Louis, his white teeth pressing into the skin of my wrist, and I am swamped with delight. I know I have to see him again.

It is like a miracle, but I am not sure who listened to my secret prayers. All day, I had been vaguely imagining escape as a bus ride to Orlando or a weekend in Cape May. Regular wishes and normal bets: *After I finish this grounding, I will ask the parents to send me to soccer camp with Kathlyn. If I bring those Goodwill bags to Mr. DePass, maybe I can get enough money to take a train up to Boston, to visit Uncle Nelson. Maybe Louis could come with me.*

But I had never dared to imagine that the next day's mail might hold those tickets. The letter's plastic window is addressed to Geneva and me, but Geneva, who almost never gets mail, swipes the envelope from my hand.

"Give that back," I say, racing after her into the house. "It came to both of us."

"We're going!" she yelps as she disappears into the dining room. I am right at her heels.

Geneva is squeaking like a puppy's chew toy as she hops around the dining room table, her hands clamped to her cheeks like those people in the Publisher's Clearing House commercials.

"Come on, what is that? Let me see."

"I knew it, I knew it. My fortune came true after all! Shows how much you know!"

"Let me see!"

She slides the envelope across the table. "We have to tell Annie," she says, and heads through the swinging door into the kitchen.

I pull out and unfold a packet of our matching itineraries, a computer printout of seat numbers and departure information, and lastly, two pairs of tickets. An expanding bubble of excitement begins to fill my stomach.

"Hey, where is she?" Geneva calls. When I follow her into the kitchen, Geneva is staring at the wall. I follow her gaze to a blue-chalked word that reminds me of my own hyperlegible handwriting, the bobbing *A* and *o*, and the same three-fingered capital *M*s that I make.

"Who's Moma?"

"No, it's MoMA. The Museum of Modern Art. Remember when Dad took us there a few years ago? To see those paintings by Van Gogh?" Geneva's face is blank. "I can't believe you forgot, you hated this story. He was the artist who cut off his ear. He died penniless, but today one painting is worth more money than like, . . . how much a grand-prize winner gets on *Jeopardy*. More, maybe. Go, get your jacket. We'll take a subway if you feel up to it."

"His own ear? He cut off his own ear? I think I'm going to be sick."

"Yep, that's what you said last time."

She does not move. "Besides, you're grounded."

I regard my sister thoughtfully. Mom's words clatter in my ear. "You have to set a good example for your sister, Holland. Geneva looks up to you." Then the lyrics of a new bet melt through me, a coaxing strain like a cobra charmer's flute. *If you break the rule this once, you can ground yourself an extra day at the end of the week. Take a day, give a day. Take one, give one back. Nobody will know.*

"I'll add another grounded day to the end of the week," I tell Geneva confidently. "Annie is asking us to come, otherwise she wouldn't have told us where she is, so it must be important.

Plus I want to show her these tickets. Now, can you manage the subway? If not, we have to pool for cab fare."

"I guess I can do it," Geneva says. "The subway's quicker, and I don't want to miss Annie."

She does not make a sound during the entire six stop ride up to the museum. Her face loses all expression and color, especially when a huge crowd swells inside the car once we hit Times Square, and she is first out the door when we arrive at our stop on Fifty-third and Fifth. She mouths a string of Hail Marys but she does not peep.

"You did it," I say when we emerge into the swarming street.

"Barely," she breathes.

"You're just being dramatic," I say. "You were way better than *barely*."

We use Dad's University membership card to get into the museum for half price. Automatically, I head to the permanent collection, and I spy Annie before Geneva does. The back of her bright head and shoulders blocks a chunk of my view of *Starry Night*, and I wonder how long she has been standing there. People jostle around the paintings, but Annie stands still as a spike through the floor.

"This painting makes me hungry," she says

with a sigh as soon as we are close enough to hear. "You know what I like best about it? I like how he signed his first name. It makes him seem approachable, like you could have walked down the road to his house and shared coffee with him, borrowed sugar from him, exchanged paintbrushes. 'Trade you a stippling sponge for a camel mop.' Easy as that."

"Where have you been?" Geneva gasps. "Holland got in big trouble when she invited Louis over, like you told her. She took your advice and broke the 'no guests without permission' rule and got caught. She's grounded, she shouldn't even be here. But I can, since all I was doing was painting my bird."

"Be quiet, Geneva."

"Some things are more important than rules," Annie says. Her eyes sparkle, and she smells nice, like a freshly sharpened pencil, but her wrinkled dress and blazer hang too large over the narrow outline of her body, and one of her shoe straps has come undone. It quivers and flicks along the floor like the tongue of a snake, and it makes her look untidy and distracted. I wonder if other museum patrons mistake her for a homeless person. It would explain their lack of communication with her, their refusal to make eye contact. Yet Annie seems comfortably unaware of herself and the people around her.

"We need to put these colors in the kitchen," she says as she turns back to the painting. "You can't find these hues anywhere in a city landscape."

"In summer you can," I say, loyal to my New York. "Especially in Central Park. But look here, Annie. Look what came in the mail today." I remove the envelope from my jacket pocket and show her the tickets.

"Cripes, how'd you get those?" Annie asks. "There's some luck, a free vacation."

Geneva begins hopping around us in a circle. "We're going to Saint Germaine! We're going, we're going, we're going!"

"You ordered them for us, didn't you?" I say.

"Holland, really. How would I get the money to send you two off to the Caribbean for a weekend?"

"It's a freebie!" Geneva shouts. "A freebie, period! A hooky trip."

"Geneva, you're about to get smacked." I slip the tickets back in my pocket. I can hardly bear to look at them, they delight me so much. "But it's not free, Annie. Plane tickets don't just show up in the mail. There's no receipt. Maybe they aren't even paid for. I don't think the parents will let us go."

"Mmmph," says Annie. She lifts her hand to her chin, as if thinking. I notice that her nails are brightly caked with paint.

"So," I say impatiently, "I guess what I'm asking is what would you do?"

"What would I do? I wouldn't tell a soul." Annie smirks like the delinquent kid she probably once was. "I'd cut school Friday, cab to the airport, jump on the plane, and figure out the rest of my plan once I got to the island." It is the most irresponsible advice I have heard from a grown-up since Uncle Nelson told me to stand on my head when I did math problems because it supplied more blood to brain neurons. I couldn't tell if he was kidding, and now I don't know if Annie is either. Geneva's chant of "Yes! Yes!" does not help me to think logically.

"The parents would worry if we didn't tell them."

"You could always phone them once you're there," Annie responds with a shrug. "Seems like you're making a pretty big deal out of a pretty small one."

The thick, oily stars of *Starry Night* bulge from their canvas like a handful of gooey butterscotch candies. Tempting.

"Anyway, I'm thirsty, I need a cup of coffee." Annie touches her fingers to her neck, hopping back and forth on her feet in the graceless, childish way that has grown familiar to me. *Slsp, slsp* goes her loose shoe strap, a sound that troubles me because it is a falling-apart noise, like a broken muffler or a leaky faucet. "I'm off to the cafeteria. If there's time, you should take a look at the iron sculpture show on the third floor." She begins to glide away.

"Wait, Annie . . ."

She does not turn around. I watch her breeze through the crowd, her long blue skirt flowing out behind her like a peel of night sky.

After she's gone, I turn to my sister. "Listen, Geneva, you realize we need to get the parents' permission to go away."

"Please don't ask them, please! You're grounded, remember? They'll never let us go. Don't ruin it by asking, we can take care of ourselves, please—"

"Stop whining, it makes it harder for me to figure out what to do. Just simmer down until I think of a plan. Deal?"

Geneva sighs, but nods. "Deal."

We step hesitantly around the gallery while we wait for Annie to return from her coffee break. "Annie didn't look so good today," Geneva finally volunteers.

"Yeah, I noticed. Like she has a flu," I say.

"Or she's just tired," Geneva muses.

"Well, she definitely gets tired of us," I admit. "Like that day she just abandoned us in Soho. She is not the best example of a guardian."

"She's not any worse example than *you*," Geneva contests. "You're both alike, come to think of it. Like how you traded your school coat, and Louis coming over, and you yelling at Mom. I could imagine Annie doing all those things when she was a kid."

"I don't want to be a bad example for you," I say honestly.

"Oh, I like when people are bad examples," Geneva assures me.

We roam through the different rooms, then move up to the third floor where we stare at artwork until our eyes are stunned by colors and figures.

Then I look at Geneva; we are thinking the same thing. "She's not coming back," I say. "The old Annie disappearing act. Let's go before the parents get home and find out we're not there."

"I tried calling you girls this afternoon," Dad says absently that night at dinner. He reaches for a bowl of creamed parsnips and lands a spoon-ful onto his plate. "The Deli does these rather well, I think," he says to Mom.

"Sixth sense with the garlic," Mom adds. They detour into a tranquil discussion about their various favorite Deli specialties, and I think Dad has forgotten about trying to call home, but like a reliable boat he tacks back on course and says, in the same casual voice, "Didn't you hear the phone, Holland? When I rang earlier today?"

My heart upshifts a speed. "No, but we were here. I don't know how that happened."

"Because we were in the cellar, " Geneva says. "Looking for old pottery crocks. They make good paint mixers as long as there's no hole in the bottom. But remember, Holland, when I thought I heard the phone? Remember when I said, 'Do you hear the phone ringing?'"

"Yep, and you were right. I couldn't hear a thing, but it was probably you calling, Dad."

We spread on lies like frosting, adding smiles and politeness for extra sweetness.

"Wasn't *Annie* around again today? She could have picked up the phone." Mom's voice is more insistent than Dad's as she takes the helm of the questioning.

"She was here yesterday but not today,"

Geneva says. "She's really busy. But she lets us work on the mural when she isn't here. We're her apprentices."

"She does a good job, too," I say. "She's very professional and responsible."

"I'm sure she is." Dad looks at Mom.

"Annie can't be allowed too much responsibility," Mom says pointedly.

"Free artistic rein has its benefits," Dad responds. "And there has been no damage as of yet, Lydia."

They are talking in a parent code. Geneva senses it, too.

"Have you both met Annie?" she blurts out.

"Certainly, " Dad says. "A charming young person. Very level-headed."

"A good example, isn't that what you said, Quentin?" Mom asks in a stagy voice. "You said she would be a good role model for our girls."

I feel the smothered meaning in their words and I am irritated at being excluded.

The sudden chime of the doorbell causes us all to flinch.

"Speaking of which," Mom says with a smile, "we have guests tonight."

Dad jumps up from his seat. "Hail, hail," he says. "The Hills are here!" He claps his hands and leaves the dining room to answer the door.

"You're not serious," I begin. Mom's smile wilts.

"Oh, chin up," she says, her hands twiddling her necklace. "I won't embarrass you, Holland. Trust me." She lifts her eyes from me to the doorway. "Well, hello, all!"

"Lydia, oh, Lydia!" Mr. Hill's voice booms Mom's name in song.

I do not turn around, even when I hear Aaron Hill say, "Hey, Holland."

Instead, I stare straight into my plate, gritting my teeth together, wondering what words will come out if I do trust myself to speak.

"Hey, Geneva," Aaron says. "We brought cake."

"Why don't the old folks separate into the living room?" Dad says. "Who would like tea?"

Geneva rolls her eyes up at the ceiling. I stand.

"Hi, Aaron." Be polite. It's not his fault. "I'm not feeling very well. If you'll excuse me, I'm going upstairs."

"How's school, Aaron? How's fencing?" Geneva asks, trying to distract him on my account. "What flavor cake did you bring?"

"Uh, fine. Uh, lemon." Aaron's head bobs from Geneva to me and back again. He is wearing a coat and tie, and his hair is beginning to bounce out of its damp combing. It is easy to see from his obedient expression why Bishop Brown kids call him Aaron the Pious. I feel sorry for him, but not enough to want to stick around and be friendly.

"'Scuse me." I slide past Aaron and pound up the stairs to my bedroom, where I sit, waiting, on the edge of my bed, squeezing my knees in my hands. How unfair and controlling of the parents to do this, to deliver a boyfriend straight to the front door, packaged and tied like the box of lemon cake he walked in with.

After a few minutes I hear the brisk tap of Mom's heels up the stairs.

If you don't let yourself get talked into going downstairs, then you should . . . you better . . . you have to . . . I can't even think of what to bet myself.

"Bets don't really work anyway," I mutter just as Mom opens the door.

"What's that?" she asks.

"I said, I wish you would knock before you barge in my room."

Mom folds her arms across her chest and leans forward over them. The position makes her body appear disfigured, as if she were a statue that had been broken and reglued crooked. "As long as we're making wish lists, then I wish you would stop being rude and come downstairs to entertain our guests."

"I don't feel good."

"You were fine a few minutes ago. You ate all your dinner."

"Aaron Hill must have made me sick, then." I force myself to look into Mom's eyes.

"What is the matter with you, Holland? Why are you acting so childish?"

"You never even gave Louis a chance."

"This has nothing to do with Louis. This is about being polite to the Hills."

"If you like Aaron so much, then you go out with him."

"Sweetheart, I'm not saying you ought to go out with Aaron. My only thought was that here's this young man, a dear friend of yours from childhood—maybe you don't remember but Angie and I do—and if you stopped being so stubborn for a minute—"

"Did you ever meet Elizabeth's boyfriend?" I ask. Mom steps back, closer to the door.

"Oh, Holland, you do choose your moments. You're as churlish as Geneva these days."

"Didn't she have boyfriends? Did you pick them out? She was my big sister. I have a right to know."

My mother sighs and raises a hand to her

face, using her thumb and forefinger to smooth out the waxed arcs of her eyebrows, as if by doing so she can fix her expression into a state of unfurrowed composure. "We will talk about Elizabeth later if you like, but I am simply not in the mood for this while our guests are downstairs."

"Your guests, you mean."

Mom takes a steadying breath. "First losing your school jacket, then this business with that boy, Louis, in your *room* no less, and I know you and your sister weren't here today after school. What has gotten into you lately? Originally your father's and my position with *Annie* was that it would be helpful for you girls somehow, but the situation obviously is not coming right."

"What position? What situation?"

"Oh, please. This kitchen, the painting, it's all pure indulgence. Do you think I just fell off the turnip truck?"

I picture Mom, sitting cross-legged and frowning in a farmer's turnip truck.

"Why are you smirking at me?" she asks.

"I wasn't smirking."

"What is happening to you?" Mom asks softly. "Where is the sweet and loving girl I know, who takes care of herself and her sister? What happened to her?"

"I am taking care of us!" I say, and although

Mom glances automatically at the door to make sure it is closed, I do not lower my voice. "I'm just taking care of us in a different way now!"

"I see," she says. "You don't think Dad and I know what we're doing, that's it? You're trying to make us feel guilty because we both work? Because we can't be home with you girls every minute of the day?"

"You know that's not it. I'm proud of Dad's and your jobs."

"Then make *me* proud tonight. Come downstairs to say hello to the Hills, who are dear old friends of ours."

There is no way for me to explain why I cannot go downstairs and entertain Aaron Hill. I can't find the words to bridge the distance between Mom and me, and so I am silent.

"I take it you won't be coming down, will you?" she says finally.

I shake my head.

"Well, I hope you can rest easy with this behavior on your conscience, Holland." Mom's voice is considerably chilled. "Because I know I couldn't."

"You never told me his name."

"Whose name?"

"Elizabeth's boyfriend. What was his name?"

"He went to Bishop Brown." Mom keeps

her voice cool and composed, although I am sure the question disturbs her. "I don't know where he is these days. He lost touch with us not long after. His name was William."

"William," I repeat. She nods and for a second I wonder how my mother sees me, my face puckered and glaring, my clenched fists. I doubt I'll ever know what emotions lie behind her smoothed eyebrows and balanced voice.

"We'll talk later," she says.

I think I will cry once she closes the door and I hear her shoes clicking down the stairs. But once she is gone, I do not feel like crying at all. In fact, I feel light-headed, almost joyful. I lie down on my bed and my fingers find the envelope tucked under my pillow. I close my eyes and picture an immense warm blue sky, and the image is a shock of freedom.

saint jude

I sit on the roof, waiting. The night air is chilly, there are no stars, and the moon is quilted under layers of clouds.

When I saw Louis at the vendor this morning, my problems uncorked, releasing a flood of talk I was not sure I wanted to share. With my eyes on Geneva, who walked ahead of us making wide circles around the pigeons she so detests, I began with the story of the other Shepards and ended by telling Louis about the plane tickets under my pillow. My speech was two avenue blocks long, but Louis was a listening, sympathetic audience.

"Let me come over and see you tonight," he said.

"Except you're indefinitely banned from my house."

"You got a roof and a way to get up?"

I nodded. "There's a fire ladder."

"Done. Be on the roof at eight and watch for me. We can hang out together, in private."

"Isn't that dangerous? Won't you be riding the subway awfully late?"

"No, I'll just sleep over at my uncle Pete's. He lives in Chelsea." Louis made a fist and tapped it against my nose. "See you."

He lets me know he's here by throwing something at the streetlight in front of our house. I lean over the tarpaulin-tacked wall and spy his shadow.

"Psst! I'm up here."

"Rapunzel, Rapunzel!" Louis talks so loud that my stomach tenses, and I cross my fingers against anybody inside the house hearing us.

"You're an outlaw in this town," I say when Louis swings up over the wall. "Charged with the crime of being in my bedroom last week."

"Of kissing you in your bedroom last week,"

Louis corrects. His knees brush against mine as he slides next to me. Hearing him say the word *kissing* makes me look away.

"So Aaron the Pious is allowed in the house, and I'm lower than a roach or something." He smiles and leans back, his laced fingers making a hammock to hold his head. "Don't tell your mom, but once a house gets roaches, there's no getting rid of them."

I used to think I would never be able to come up with more than a dozen original words to say to Louis Littlebird, but we talk for a long time. There is something about Louis's voice, although it is hardly familiar, that lets me loosen the wrappings I hold around my outside self.

It is not just me talking, either. Louis tells me things: about how last year he and his sister took their old dog, Rosie, to the vet and how he held her and hugged her while the vet gave Rosie the shot to put her to sleep, and how he cried for three days. We talk about Matthew versus Geneva, and I have to admit that Matthew's biting sounds like a worse problem than Geneva's wild dreams, although Louis is stumped when I tell him that Geneva has threatened to cut off her own tongue if we don't get to go to Saint Germaine.

"I think she stole the concept from Van Gogh," I explain. "She sort of likes to talk about things that also make her sick."

Louis laughs. "A mute sister isn't the worst punishment in the world. If Mattie shut up for more than five minutes I'd consider it a blessed miracle." His face becomes more serious. "You're going, aren't you? To Saint Germaine?"

"It feels funny to say yes. It breaks a lot of rules. I'm not honoring my mom and dad's wishes, I'm lying, I'm stealing."

"Come on, you aren't stealing anything. It's only a matter of time before someone admits to buying those tickets for you."

"I guess." In the week I have grown to know him, I have had to recategorize Louis from the stranger of my daydreams into reality, and even his physical appearance has altered from the shift. His eyes, which at first had seemed so aloof, are eyes that cried over his dog. The hands he uses to pin wrestling opponents also know how to give his mom neck rubs.

"Besides, it seems like you two can pretty much take care of yourselves. I mean, when I saw your mom that day, no offense but I thought she was your grandmother," Louis says. "She looked so flimsy, like she'd crumble into dust if I slammed the door too hard. Tonight at dinner,

I asked my mom what she would do if three of her own kids were, you know, were gone, just like that. She said it's the kind of tragedy that's toughest on the parents. She said men in white coats would have to carry her away."

"My mom's strong, even if she doesn't look it," I say. "She's a survivor. That doesn't mean that on the inside she isn't grieving. It's only that she has a different way—"

"Stop right there, because I didn't mean to get you uptight, okay?"

"She's not crazy, you know. Neither of them is crazy. They're regular parents, maybe quieter and older, maybe a little more cautious—"

"Hey, I'm sorry!" Louis didn't mean to speak so loud; now his voice sinks into a whisper. "I'm sorry."

We are both quiet, searching for the right thing to say. "There's this tour that goes past our house every Saturday," I begin after a moment. "Over the years, the guides have changed, but the tour always ends with the same old story, about how some old mayor of New York's mistress lived in our house and how sometimes you can see the mayor's ghost creeping down our front steps. It's the highlight of the tour. No one pays attention to the other facts, like that our street is crooked because it used to be a cow path, or that it's one of the only houses in the Village with a cellar. It's the ghost story that grabs them. They love it." I sigh, linking my arms around my knees like a basket handle to hold myself. "And that's what's wrong with our family."

"Wow, you lost me," Louis says. "What does some mayor's ghost have to do with anything?"

"Because I'm a ghost story, too," I say. "Geneva and me both. And our story is so awful that it crowds out everything else about us. Whatever else Geneva and I are—a good tennis player or an artist—has been swallowed up by our haunting. And you know the worst part? We never even knew them. We never shared their history. We live inside our very own haunted house, and we have no idea who the ghosts are, any more than we can remember the mayor and his mistress."

"Yeah," Louis says. He reaches his arm around my neck, and his fingers are warm, kneading my skin. "I get what you mean. Even my mom had heard the story of your family. My oldest brother, Francis, was three grades under your brother John. Mom said they were on the debate team together, and once she watched them debate against Xavier. I asked if she remembered him, and she told me your brother had a loud debating voice, one of the only people she could hear from where she was sitting in the back row because she was pregnant and liked to be near the exit."

I smile; other people have talked about John's public speaking voice, how he liked to get his point across in crashing decibels.

"I also asked my mom what she would do if a ticket to Saint Germaine dropped in her lap," Louis continues. "Guess what she said?"

"What?" I lift my shoulders. "I give up."

"She said, 'I'd think someone up there was watching over me.'"

"Is that what you think?"

Louis uses his free hand to scoop something from the pocket of his leather jacket. "Here, give me your hand," he says.

"What is this?" I cannot see, I can only feel the nugget of weight he places in the palm I offer him.

"It's Saint Jude," Louis tells me.

"What's he the saint of?"

"I think he's the saint of travel. You should take him with you to Saint Germaine. He'll keep you protected."

I almost want to laugh in Louis's face, he sounds and looks so trusting and earnest, but instead I quickly drop my head to scrutinize the tiny tin statue, no bigger than a Crackerjack prize. Then I lift Saint Jude to my ear, like a shell.

"He's saying, 'Remember to take sunblock.'" Louis smiles. His hand on my shoulder anchors me to him. "He's saying, keep safe and come back in one piece."

"Is he?"

"Yeah." The second kiss Louis Littlebird gives me feels like slow motion, as if he had decided on it long before he climbed up onto this roof tonight. At first my face and body are stiff, and I keep waiting for him to figure out that I haven't had any experience with kissing, but soon I realize that it comes pretty naturally to me. The sign of a genuine Ick, I guess.

Suddenly the moon makes its debut, throwing white light over us, making me shy.

"It's getting late, probably," I say. "I bet it's almost eleven."

"Yeah, I should get going. I'll see you tomorrow morning." We stand together, and he kisses me quickly on the cheek, a velvety soft brush that is nothing like a night crawler.

"Goodnight."

"'Night, Louis."

He swings down the ladder with an athlete's ease. By the cloudy, apple juice light of the street lamps, I watch him, a long shadow with a confident stroll, until he vanishes.

The tickets are hidden under my mattress, and Saint Jude stays under my pillow. I keep thinking they might guide me to the right decision. But my Tuesday night sleep is awful, and I wake the next morning feeling as if I haven't slept at all. Geneva avoids me and I know she is terrified that I will tell the parents. Every time I look at her, I am confronted with her face of silent pleading.

Wednesday night I am exhausted, flip-flopping from side to stomach to side, drifting in and out of shallow sleep. My dreams sputter and fade and are forgotten. I wake up and hear Geneva in the bathroom. Is she running the faucet or flushing the toilet? I force my eyes closed in an effort at sleep.

My fingers find the edge of Saint Jude. He is made of metal so thin that at first I thought I could bend him between my fingers, only I tried and I can't. Behind my closed eyes is dark ocean. The water moves around and through me, and so I dive deeper, pulling myself along the current. We're swimming together, Geneva and I, and she is telling me how the water fixes her, but her words are secret, the private underwater words shared between sisters, and I am smiling now, the water rushing in between my teeth and pouring into my smile.

"Holland! Holland!"

My name. I open my eyes to see my sister standing in the doorway of my room. The light shining behind her acts as an X ray, separating her body from her nightgown.

"Holland, are you okay?

I close my eyes and open them again, but I do not wake up. I am not dreaming, but I am not awake, either. Held in this moment between sleep and consciousness, I am resolved. I know what we are supposed to do.

"I'm awake." I yawn and slither up in bed.

"You were talking real loud. I couldn't understand what you were saying. It must have been a dream." Geneva approaches me reluctantly. "You need me to sing or hear prayers or anything?"

"Geneva," I say slowly. "I am going to ask you a question and you must answer honestly. Think hard and take your time. How scared would you be to get on a plane?"

She is even frightened of the question. I can see by the way her body collapses slightly around her middle, shoulders drooping and knees bending to give way to the disintegrating support of her stomach.

"Very," she answers. "Very very. As many *very*s as you can say in three hours and twenty minutes. But I'd do it. I'd do it if I knew that Saint Germaine was waiting for me at the end."

When we come home from school on Thursday afternoon, the kitchen looks wild, framed by colors never before introduced into our house. I have been a helper to the process, a reliable mixer of varnishes, a steady hand at stippling the mattes of the sky and ocean. Geneva and Annie are the real artists. As soon as she drops her book bag, Geneva is at the sink, where she begins to mix paints and thinners with the expertise of a chef.

They have been painting the sky as a storm front, "because the colors are more funky," Geneva informs me, using a word I know she borrowed from Annie. And so our walls shine oyster gray and sulfurous yellow, ribboned with hints of pink and lavender and misted with cloud tatters.

"On the ceiling you should paint Zeus, holding a giant lightning bolt ready to strike down anyone using too much basil," I joke. "Since it's a kitchen," I explain, when neither Annie nor Geneva laughs. Geneva dips her brush and scrutinizes its color.

"Does this look too mustardy?" she asks me, holding the tip of her brush. "Maybe more linseed oil," she says, answering her own question.

Annie is crouched on the floor, mixing paints into pottery saucers. "Take off your funny hat, Holland, and get working," she says, looking up at me. Her face is bright with cheery flecks of paint, but grape-dark shadows are scooped beneath her eyes, and her linen blazer seems to engulf her body.

I stoop next to Annie. She hands me a bristle brush and a dish of brown goop.

"Are you shrinking, or are your clothes growing?" I ask her, half-kidding.

"Add a little more ochre and mix until it's even," Annie says. "It's for shading the tree trunk."

"You look tired. Might be spring flu. It's going around," I say. "There were four kids absent in my class today."

"Holland, if I'm here to help you, what's the use of your trying to help me? We just cancel each other out." It is the first time Annie has admitted she came into our home for any other reason than to paint the walls, and her comment takes me by surprise.

"Okay," I say. "Forget it. Take care of yourself."

"Thanks."

"We're going," I say after a minute. I squirt a dollop of ochre yellow paint into the saucer, like melting butter into chocolate, and wait for her reaction. None comes. "Tomorrow," I continue. "We're cutting school at lunch. We're not telling anybody. Other than you, I mean. And Louis. And I'll tell the parents, too, once we're on our way." It was my final bet to myself. *If you can get yourself to that island, you have to let the parents know. It's not fair to worry them.*

Annie sits back on her heels, touching her fingers against the hollow of her neck. We lapse into a silence so long that I think she is angry with me. I draw my face up, defiant, waiting.

"Well, Holland Shepard," she says finally through a little laugh, "you have more spirit than I'd figured. You're turning into someone I can really relate to."

Her words make me so happy I could hug her, if she were the hugging type.

saint germaine ten

I sink my spoon into the molded plastic compartment of chocolate pudding, which looks like a square of wet cardboard and tastes not much better. I turn away from lunch to gaze at my view, so clear it is as if the window itself had been painted blue.

Geneva has worn herself out with Hail Marys and is working through a string of Pledge of Allegiances. When I lean forward I can see that her body is pushed up into her chair, head and shoulders glued to the back of the seat, giving her the appearance of an astronaut just

launched into space. Only her mouth moves—
"antoo the republic forwidget stans . . ."

"Do you want your crackers?" I ask.
Without turning her head, she flips the package
onto my tray.

Neither of us has brought books, so I busy
myself with the travel magazines stacked inside
the netted pocket attached to the back of the
seat in front of mine, then turn my attention
again to the window. The view, though
unchanging, exhilarates me. "We will be cruis-
ing at an altitude of 28,000 feet," the pilot had
informed us over the speakers. A breathless
height.

So far, I have enjoyed everything about this
trip, especially the airport, with its cargo-sized
elevators and free-standing lounges and endless
glass terminals through which you can see
landed planes idling like slow-moving beasts in
a game park. Even the taste of packaged food
and the hum of packaged air is flavored with
adventure and chance.

Getting to this point, all the way up here to
become a dot in the sky, had not been so difficult, not nearly as hard as I had thought it
would be once I knew we were going. The den-
tist's notes had been easy; only the most critical
eye could tell my imitation of Mom's skinny,

long-tailed handwriting from the real thing. The train ride was quick and efficient. Check-in offered only a few uncertain moments when, filling out our unaccompanied minor forms, I was faced with having to list the names of who would be picking us up and supervising our stay on the island. I hesitated before printing Ryan and Dana Hubbard. As the check-in clerk took the forms, briskly stapling them to our tickets without a second look at the parents' forged signatures, I remembered what Annie had said about people being too busy with their own lives to care about anyone else's. She might have been right, but it's a lonely vision, a city filled with people who see right past or through you as long as you seem to play by the rules and don't make trouble.

I phoned the parents the moment before our seats were called for boarding. Dad's voice sounded lonely and long distance, as if he already knew I would be disappointing him. "Leave a message and we'll be glad to return your call."

"Hi, it's Holland. Look, this is hard to explain, but Geneva and I are going away for the weekend. We're fine, we're safe, I'm sorry, but we're going to Saint Germaine. To our house. We'll be back Sunday night, I'm sorry, again. I love you. I promise I'll be grounded when we get back."

After hanging up, I moved far away from the phone, retreating to another part of the airport lounge to resist calling the parents again and apologizing a few more times before takeoff.

"I love to travel," I say to Geneva now, pressing my nose against the plane window. "Love it, love it, love it."

"How much longer till we get down? My head hurts from the altitude. I might be dehydrating."

"Geneva, you act like we're hang-gliding to get there."

"I can't help getting airsick, especially since you made me take the aisle."

"You said you *wanted* the aisle."

"I need to find the bathroom," she says. She unhinges from her seat with the stiff joints of a marionette. I watch her careful progress up the aisle before returning to stare at my sky.

When we met at our vendor this morning, Louis told me not to forget my camera.

"I don't own a camera," I said, surprised. I hadn't even thought of it.

"Aw, man, if I'd known I would have lent you mine," Louis said.

"Really," I answered, "it's no big deal." What Louis didn't know was that I wouldn't have taken a camera even if I did own one. I'd seen enough glossy, eternalized moments of Saint Germaine, and I don't want to capture more of them. For the past couple of days, I have been electric with impulse, like the person who rushes headlong into the picture just before the flash goes off. I do not want to think about consequences.

I smile into the blue window and my smile is defiant: I am here, too, it says. I have a right.

Geneva returns a few minutes later, all eyes.

"You look like you saw a Martian."

"Did you know all along?" she gasps. "Why didn't you say anything?"

"Know what? Say what?"

"That Annie is on our plane! Why didn't you tell me?"

"No! She is? I didn't know." I lift out of my seat and crane my neck, trying to locate Annie among the hills of heads bumped over their seat backs.

"In front." Geneva points. "She's sleeping. I'm not kidding. Go look."

A movie has started and I walk, half-crouched up the aisle, to where I find her within the vague radius Geneva indicated, asleep on the aisle seat of the third row.

She is tented by her blazer, a deflated crumple across her shoulders and chest. In sleep she is fixed and distant as a star. Her nostrils do not dent in sleep-breath, her body makes no stir. Yet her presence is more assuring to me than the guarantee of any inflatable life raft or seat that doubles as a flotation device.

"Annie," I whisper. The man next to her looks up at me, scowling. He is wearing headphones and he points to the movie.

"Shhh."

"Annie!" I say louder. She opens her eyes; their gray is only a saucer's overlay around sleep-dark pupils, and her face looks tired, soft enough to smudge with the barest press of a finger.

"See, I'm your warden after all," she says in the secret voice.

"You didn't have to come," I say, although I am sure relief beams over my face. "Why did you come? You look so tired." So sick.

"Mmmph. I'm just doing my job, delivering you safely."

"Do the parents know?"

Annie snaps her eyes shut and turns her head away from me. I can see there's no point trying to work more words out of her.

"You're right," I say wonderingly when I rejoin my sister. "She's up front. I can't figure out how she sneaked on. We never saw her in the terminal or anywhere. She says she wants to make sure we get there safely. She looks pretty worn out, though, and none of the flight attendants even thought to give her a blanket."

"Oh, other people don't notice her," Geneva says.

"What do you mean?"

"I mean they don't pay attention to her. We see her in our own way, but everyone else?" Geneva flicks the air. "No one notices. No one knows how to look."

I try to watch more carefully how people observe Annie once we deplane and are faced with the bleak airstrip of the main island, but as far as I can tell nobody really reacts to any of us.

All our bags are carry-on, so we don't have to wait beside the carousel in the baggage claim. Annie has slid into her broken strap shoes and does not remove her blazer, although Geneva and I ball our own jackets into our bags as soon as the air, warm as a bakery, hits our faces. The setting sun hurts my eyes. My watch reads 6:21 P.M.

"We're here at last," Geneva says, stretching

her pale, bare arms over her head. "My fortune came true. I knew it would."

"We're not there yet. We need a car to take us to our launch site," Annie reminds her as we walk out into the nearly empty airport parking lot. Other passengers are staggering into the heated air, waving for the few available car services to pick them up. "That guy over there, standing next to the Range Rover. Geneva, go ask."

The man, a native of the main island, tells us his name is Chad.

"I can drive you to Regina Beach, then you wait for the boat to take you over," he says, opening the doors of his spotlessly clean car. The interior smells like an entire can of air freshener was recently unleashed into it. "Thirty minutes to Saint Germaine, twenty minutes to Clothilde, forty-five minutes to Moore Island by motorboat. If you take a sailboat, a bit longer. Where are you going?"

"Saint Germaine," I say.

"As I was going to Saint Germaine," Geneva recites giddily, bouncing on her seat, "I met a man with seven brains. And every brain had seven pains, and every pain had seven—"

"What are you talking about? Calm down!" I scold her. "There are days I wish you *would* slice off your tongue."

Instead she sticks it out at me, but I am relieved that she is more enthusiastic than unnerved by the new surroundings. In fact, for a day of traveling she has done remarkably well.

We are here at last. I roll down my window and am wrapped in arid air. The troubles that bound me all morning; the lies I told my teachers, the shrinking sock-wad of bills that I've paid out for cab and train fares, the bolt of chaos that will be striking 176 Waverly Place any second—slowly release their hold.

The setting sun is bleeding its orange and grapefruit and cranberry juice colors into the sky. We drive past walls of sugar cane, a clutch of goats all tied together by one long rope, a man selling painted coconut shells. We pass a row of cement houses and a cemetery of crooked crosses. I close my eyes and the Range Rover seems to gather speed, hurtling us faster and faster down the road, so fast that we melt into a ball of red fire roaring through the green cane. My heart shudders in my chest and my hands are a fusion of salty, wet fingers. I open my eyes; I remember to breathe. The colors of the island are so beautiful, they hurt.

Annie sleeps between us. Her arms, still freckled with the paint of our kitchen mural, rest on her lap. She does not open her eyes until we have arrived at Regina Beach.

She is right—it is romantic, more romantic than the Jersey shore. Pale surf breaks over a stretch of blond sand, nearly deserted save a rickety free-standing pier, a few forgotten canvas deck chairs, and a couple of fat, bright-eyed seagulls. They pick up their feet in a jerking march, sometimes heaving their bodies into a couple yards of flight before dropping back to earth. As I climb from the car, I open my mouth to taste the cool salt air. Geneva, a shoe in each hand, runs to the edge of the water, testing it.

"There's our chariot," Annie says, pointing.

My eyes locate the white sliver bobbing in the waves. Slowly it shapes into a weather-beaten hull canopied by a grimy sail and crewed by two old men wearing floppy hats and all-weather oilskin jackets.

Annie waves and breaks away from us, climbing up the pier, then easily springing from pier to boat. In the setting sun, her hair is the color of gold fire. "Come on, girls," she calls. "No chickens. That means you, Geneva."

As the boat laps to the edge of the pier, one of the men reaches forward and plants a foot on its outermost lip while his other leg, heavy with muscle and burnt by sun, anchors him to the boat deck. He takes my hand as I leap, and in another second my bare feet hit the wet deck of the boat. In an instant, Geneva is beside me. Her face is serious but her eyes gleam with her own bravery.

"You did it, you did it." I scratch the back of her neck, pat her arm. We squat together in the trunk, the back of the boat, braced against the swinging jib and yardarm. Annie stays up on the other end and seems fueled by some second strength, although she looks light enough to fly away, a scrap of blue skipping over the pale waves.

I touch my jeans pocket to feel the hard lump of Saint Jude. Louis had asked me to try remembering everything I see, to report back. I look at the water and wonder if there is anything in New York City that matches all these colors.

The boat catches a puff and begins to lift and dip us over the thumping waves so carelessly I think that Annie and the men have lost control of us. We lift, sink, lift, and then a coastline of black rock and thick columns of banana trees ring our horizon.

"Volcano Beach," Annie tells us. "Those rocks you're looking at are the fossilized remains of a natural disaster that happened over a million years ago."

The giant rocks resemble half-melted candles, too fixed in place and too ancient to remind me of disaster, like the oldest black-habited nuns at Ambrose, who look harmless but are quick to slap you a demerit for tiny offenses like wearing boxer shorts beneath your kilt.

"Okay, guys, our ride's over. Out, out, before this thing beaches. Take your shoes and bags and jump."

"Into the water?" Geneva cringes and looks to me for help. "Jellyfish?" she mouths her fears to me. "Manta rays?"

"You'll be fine," I mouth back. I grab my waterlogged loafers.

Annie already has jumped overboard. She stands up to her waist in water. "Hold your bags above your heads," she tells us. I wind the strap of my carry-on tightly over my shoulder so that it tucks just beneath my armpit. Geneva copies me.

"Get your feet ready to hit bottom," Annie instructs. "It's not all that deep."

"Thanks," I say to one of the men. He smiles with teeth that catch me off guard, they are so white and sharp, and I realize that his face is not old so much as sun-leathered and salt-cured by years of winds and water.

Annie wrings out her water-sopped skirt once we are on dry land, tying a corner of the fabric into a knot that hits her at the knee. She walks quickly and her gaze is restless, her eyes like a gecko's, crisscrossing from sky to trees and back again.

"Where do we go from here?" I sigh. I am soaked and dizzy and exhausted from travel. "How far to the bungalow?"

"We're already here." Annie points. "They dropped us off at the back door, practically. Not a moment too soon."

"I don't see anything," Geneva says, but our pace quickens.

The house is wedged into a cut of hill just visible just behind a plot of banana trees. We recognize it at once, and Geneva and I break into a run, half laughing, half screaming, the way we used to on Christmas morning.

The grass rasps against my ankles, and Geneva keeps pace, for once unafraid of stepping on bullfrogs or falling down rabbit holes. Familiar objects focus and click inside my brain as I run. I spy the hammock at the edge of the lawn; its familiarity is jolting. I see the bungalow's wavy lasagna shell roof and the waist-high terra cotta pots by the door. I see the flower boxes, the slatted shutters, the two steps leading up to the patio. It is as if the box of slides have whirred together into a movie with sound and dimension. We vault the patio steps in a bound.

The tiled patio is hushed and echoing, and our breathing is heavy as horses' when we brake at the front door. We stand, unsure of our next action, until Geneva jabs at the doorbell. The sound resonates through the house with a buzz that reminds me of our mosquito zapper at the shore.

"Why are we waiting? It's not like we expect anyone to be here," Geneva says after a few panting minutes. "We need a key is all. Check under the mat. Oh!" She puts her ear against the door. "The telephone's ringing."

My fingers are warm and stain to orange when they brush over the rain-rusted key, tucked under the doormat so long that when I pick it up, its outline remains imprinted on the concrete like a tracing in a crime scene. The key sticks slightly as I turn the lock. We take off our wet shoes and socks, leaving them to dry on the patio, before stepping with caution into the darkened front room. The telephone ringing stops before we have a chance to figure out what to do about it.

"You think the parents are calling here already?" I whisper, looking at the black rotary phone.

"I don't care," Geneva says, pushing past me. "This is our house. We can be here if we want."

"Geneva, look." I point to the vase of fresh wildflowers on the coffee table. We stare at the burst of red and yellow blooms; their arrangement is like a silent invitation, a message for just my sister and me.

"We're expected," Geneva says, wide-eyed as she reaches out to touch a petal. "We're somebody's guest."

"Maybe the same person who sent us the tickets."

I move to one of the windows and pull the cord on a set of curtains. The drapes split to wash the room in twilight. The room is as sparsely decorated as a hotel lobby, more formal than the pictures, as if time has matured it into a respectable old age.

"Hey, kitchen." Geneva dashes through an arched doorway at the far end of the room. "Come look. Oh, come see this little old wooden freezer."

"In a minute." I draw each set of curtains carefully, watching the fresh dust rise from the fabric. Every window offers a smear of sunset. I squeak open the glass panes and listen to the winds snaking through the grass. I badly want to believe in all of it, I realize: the mystery tickets and the thoughtful, invisible host. I want to believe that the spirit of the island has beckoned us, enticed us with its hint of making amends for our family's wrecked past.

"There's a lot of food!" Geneva calls. I hear cupboards opening and shutting. "A giant thingy of gumdrops! Have you ever heard of fig jelly? Or raspberry chutney? Think they'd mind if we tried some? There's good cereal and health cereal. Two bad flavors of ice cream in the freezer, rum raisin and pistachio, ugh. Oh, Holland, come look what I found!" The silence that follows makes me curious enough to go see. I find Geneva in a narrow pantry galley that extends off the kitchen.

A tree rises up between the two glassed-in china cupboards. Branches curl and reach over the panes and hinges. The colors look fresh and moist, and they are bumpy to the touch.

"Our tree," I say. "It's for real."

"In oils," Geneva says. "They're thick. She must have used tubes and tubes of paint."

"It's stupendously big," I say. Branch tips

scrape the ceiling. I have to step back and stand on tiptoe to see the entire creation from top to bottom.

"I like our kitchen better," Geneva remarks. "Let's go look at the bedrooms."

There are four, each with its own window and clothes closet. Geneva and I pick out adjacent bedrooms and unpack our few items of clothing. The furnishings are few and neat, but there are enough personal touches in the master bedroom—a extra towel hanging over the back of a chair, an open bottle of suntan oil on the bedside table—to indicate that other people definitely are occupying the bungalow.

"You know, Geneva, I think the Hubbards are probably here," I say, finally voicing my concern.

"No," she snaps. "They always come down in the changeover weeks between April and May. Always. We're still in the end of March."

"Well, somebody's staying here," I persist, opening the closet. "A man and woman from the look of it. Maybe it was the Hubbards who sent us the plane tickets. Maybe they're expecting us. Did you ever think of that?"

"No," Geneva answers firmly. She sits on the bed and picks up a framed photograph from the bedside table, which she hands me. I stare at a photograph of the Hubbards. It is an outdoor picture; each of them is smiling and wearing a necklace of binoculars. Their lined faces take me by surprise. In our slides, they are permanently young, closer to Brett and Carla's age than the parents'.

"Nerds," Geneva says with a sniff.

"But look how they're holding hands," I protest, although they do look kind of nerdish. "I wonder, if they are staying here, where they went off to? I hope they don't mind if we eat some of their food. I'm starved."

"Stop saying they're here." Geneva holds her hands over her ears. "It's our place, our weekend. We're not sharing it."

"Why don't you go see if Annie wants dinner?" I suggest to change the subject. "I'll see what I can cook up."

Back in the kitchen, I snap on lights and look through the drawers and cupboards. I picture myself in the slides: me holding a can opener, me filling an ice tray. I feel like an actor who half-believes in the painted scenery as I move over a stage that only appears to be real. I know we will not be able to keep up the charade for long. At best we are visitors here; at worst we are secret trespassers. And while it doesn't seem so outrageous to think that the Hubbards might have mailed us those tickets, I'm not surprised that Geneva would rather believe in the mystery.

I make soup, using canned chicken stock and packaged noodles. I find a saucepan and rinse it out, then splash in the broth. The phone begins to ring again just as I'm stirring up a batch of lemonade. I poke my wooden spoon intensely at the concentrated lemonade lumps and hum out loud until the noise stops.

"Annie doesn't want dinner of course, just her coffee." Geneva shakes the familiar paper bag of ground coffee. "She's resting on the hammock and says she wants to sleep there. She looks tired. I have to get her some extra pillows and blankets." She skips off, excited to be the nurse instead of the patient.

From the kitchen window, I watch my sister stagger out into the garden, her chin clamped over the mounds of extra bedding. She piles blankets over Annie. I can't hear their voices, but I can see Geneva's concern for Annie by the way she stands and twists her hair, scratching absently at her bug bites rather than examining them with her usual hypochondriac's intensity.

"I don't appreciate it when people who are sick say they aren't," Geneva remarks when she comes back inside.

"What about people who are never sick but always think they are?" I counter, giving her a meaningful look.

"Oh, come on, Holland, that's different," Geneva says. "Being scared is different from being sick."

After our salty chicken soup dinner, Geneva and I join Annie outside, mostly to get away from the reproachful jangle of the telephone. We stretch out on the grass beside the hammock and pick from a shared mound of gumdrops that rests on a paper towel between us. Annie is propped up with pillows, and her restless fingers trace elaborate invisible brocades on her lap. I sneak a lasting glance at her profile. The falling twilight tones down the sting of her yellow hair and gives her face a serenity I don't find there by day.

I clear my throat. "Annie, I think people might be staying here besides us."

"The Hubbards," she answers.

"Hey, wait, how do you know?" I ask. "Are you sure?"

"And where are they?" asks Geneva.

"They're out on the main island tonight. They'll be in tomorrow."

"Are you sure?" Geneva repeats my question.

Annie shakes her head as if she cannot

believe we would bother her with such doubts. "Do you think I would bring you all the way here and then abandon you both?" she asks. "That would be very careless of me."

"Only you're not leaving us," Geneva insists.

"No, I'm right here beside you," Annie answers.

Knowing that the Hubbards will arrive tomorrow depresses and relaxes me. Deep down, I guess I always knew they were here from the moment I saw the flowers on the table. I check on Geneva; her cheeks are chipmunked with gumdrops, which prevent her from talking.

"They've always seemed pretty nice, those Hubbards," I tell her. She nods and chews, grumpily resolved.

We look up at the stars and listen to the scratch of cricket song. The night air is sweet with the scent of wild roses, and I remember the perfumed woman on the elevator to Carr's. "It's just rose water, dear. You can buy it at Bigelow's." But the air tonight is nothing like her city smell.

Geneva is quiet and I think she has fallen asleep, so her voice surprises me. "It's paradise, isn't it?" she asks.

"Paradise? I don't know. It isn't like I imagined," I answer. "I thought Saint Germaine would be a place that would make me wishful, make me miss the others. But instead I feel the opposite. What's the opposite of wishful?"

Geneva thinks a moment. "Somewhereness," she says. "When you know you're in a place you belong."

I think of *Starry Night* preserved in its museum, a greasy shimmer of colors that look as if they had been painted only hours ago. Oil paints, same as Annie's tree. The mystery and peace of that painting tint my view tonight, and I wonder how two skies, separated by so much time and distance, can speak the same language. Van Gogh must have been sort of an Ick himself, to paint such a luscious sky.

"Besides, what is paradise, anyway?" I ask.

"A splendid illusion," Annie answers.

I lift my head to look at Annie. Through my sleep-heavy eyes, I see the sickle of her body stretched like a cocoon between the trunks of the two banana trees. The image wavers, holds, and blurs again. The trees' leafy roofs lift and bend in the night breeze like a lullaby.

"'Night, Annie," I yawn.

At my side, Geneva is still whispering. "I'm

not even allergic to the roses here, have you noticed? I bet it's not roses, I bet I'm allergic to the chemicals sprayed on them when they come into the city." Her voice is so quiet that I am sure it echoes only inside my head.

the hubbards
eleven

I wake up and stare, shivering, into blackness. Where am I? I shove myself to my feet, dragging a protesting Geneva up with me, then prodding her into the house. We must have been asleep on the lawn for two or three hours, and now the night has turned cold. I tuck Geneva into bed. From far away comes the nagging ring of the telephone. I grope my way into the front room and pull out the jack. Back in my bed, I fall into a long, hard sleep, the best I've had in weeks.

Geneva's tug on my hand, too early the next morning, drags me awake.

"She's gone, her bag's gone, her shoes! We're alone!" Geneva's cheeks are beet red and sleep-creased. "She abandoned us. You don't even look surprised!"

"Stop being so dramatic." I sit up in bed and pull my arm free. The morning sun has filled the room with comfortless tropical heat. "I need a large glass of juice before I can deal with you." But there is an ache in my heart when I drift outside and see that the hammock is empty. "We knew she'd leave. She's Annie. She got us here, right? She wasn't here to stay with us forever."

Geneva's forehead wrinkles and she rests a hand on her stomach. "I'm hungry. Maybe she went to get us breakfast?"

I look around me, to the pastel-colored bungalows that dot the hill like Easter eggs. "Don't plan on it." I try to appear calm, although a level of alarm begins to percolate inside me. Suddenly Saint Germaine is the middle of nowhere, a place of exotic danger, where anything could go wrong. "Annie said the Hubbards will be here later on, remember? Till then, let's find out where the tour buses are. That would be something, to explore the island. I have money."

"Or we could go swimming," Geneva

suggests, which, although it's a careless idea, seems like the more fun one.

I am tugging on my bathing suit when I hear the voice, a woman's.

"Hello! Is anybody there?"

Immediately Geneva pops into my room, hopping from foot to foot. "Hubbards!" she mouths.

"Who are you?" A woman stands in the doorway, hugely tall and a lot more glamorous than her picture. She reminds me of Cleopatra, from the cut of her heavy, dyed black hair to her white silky dress and the snaky twists of gold jewelry that weight her chest and ears and fingers. Her question shocks me, and I have to dismiss any idea that Dana Hubbard knew anything about our arrival in Saint Germaine.

"We're Holland and Geneva," says Geneva, who seems less shocked.

"W-who?" But I can tell that almost immediately she has connected and identified us, and her eyes lose their watchfulness as they move back and forth from me to my sister. "Lydia?" she whispers.

"Mom's in New York," I answer. "It's just us. Me and Geneva."

"Why aren't you here next month?" Geneva asks.

"Lydia's girls." Dana's nails, shellacked gold ovals like beetles' wings, flutter to her lips. "Holland, Geneva Shepard? This is so strange, this is so hard to believe. Oh, girls. Where's Ryan? Ryan!" She shouts his name, then to herself mutters, "Outside, he can't hear. . . . He's not going to believe . . ."

Then, before we can react, or in Geneva's case, escape, we are clamped inside the jaws of Dana Hubbard's steam-shovel grip. I quickly inhale a supply of air before my face gets squished by a generous square of shoulder pad.

"Can we have some breakfast?" Geneva asks as she staggers away to a safe distance. "We don't know where Annie went, and we're starv—"

"We know you weren't expecting us," I say, cutting off Geneva mid-demand. "And we're sorry we didn't call ahead, but you usually come down later. We thought we'd be alone here."

Dana keeps looking over her shoulder as if Ryan might appear any moment, and her sentences come out all crooked and in halves. "No, we pushed it ahead a few weeks, the warming trend and all, but your parents never. . . . I need to talk to Lydia. And Ryan, he has to . . . oh dear, just a minute." She reaches into her handbag and pulls out a handkerchief, which she uses to blow her nose. Her eyes are damp, and I feel conspicuously unemotional in contrast.

"I'm hungry," Geneva declares.

"Right." Dana clicks her nails together, as if snapping herself to action. "Let's put some breakfast in you. Food first, questions later." Then she breaks her own just-made rule by asking, "But how? How did you get here?"

"Plane," Geneva answers. "I'm actually very calm at flying. Plus, Annie was with us. The lady who painted your tree," Geneva adds. "She's a painter."

Dana raises her eyebrows. "Annie the painter. I'm not sure I've ever had the pleasure. . . . But that tree, it's a very special part of the house. Anyway, breakfast . . . eggs and potatoes. There's baking powder, which I think . . ." She squeezes my shoulders as we move out to the kitchen, and throughout the morning I notice how Dana's squeezes mark the forks in the paths of her speech.

Ryan Hubbard is outside by the back door, where he is in the process of unloading groceries from the Hubbards' car. He is huge, almost a giant, but his craggy face is softened by his thin, wire-rimmed glasses and button nose, so I am not scared to look all the way up, up, up at him. Although he does not have the kind of face that allows you to figure out exactly what he is thinking, his surprise to see us is not the angry kind. There is a second round of introductions, accompanied by hugs that make my ribs creak.

"So you don't mind that we're here?" I ask.

"Oh, we're . . ." Dana squeezes my sister, who is in closest squeezing distance. "It's a wonder, that's what it is."

"Out of the blue," Ryan adds. He gives me a bag to take into the kitchen, and from another bag lifts a bunch of orange flowers. "Glad we got these," he says, handing them to his wife, "seeing as it's a celebration kind of day now." He and Dana really do seem joyful, I realize. Their smiles are broad, their eyes wide as they look at each other and us.

"Tiger lilies!" Geneva exclaims. "They're gigantic!"

Dana tucks her hair behind her ears and begins to unbutton her gauzy sleeve cuffs, preparing herself for her role as chef. Sieves, bowls, and mixers pulled from shelves too high for me to reach begin crowding the counter.

"Who wants banana muffins?" she asks.

"Me, me, and coffee, too." Geneva points to

the coffee pot. "I know how to make it all by myself."

"Okay, chief, let's see you brew us up a pot," Ryan says.

Suddenly Dana bangs her measuring cup of flour on the counter with a noise that startles Geneva and me; as we turn to look at her, we realize the bang was on purpose. There is silence, and I have a feeling that the food-first-questions-later rule is about to be broken again.

"Why are you girls here by yourselves?" Dana crosses her arms over her chest and leans against the counter, regarding us evenly. "Why aren't your parents with you? Do they know where you are?"

If I look at Geneva, I know I'll want to lie, so I keep my eyes on Dana as I answer. "They do now. I left them a message from the airport yesterday. We didn't exactly let them in on our plans until we knew they couldn't stop us."

"Oh, Lord. I have to call," Dana says to Ryan, using the low, grim voice of adult responsibility.

"Wait," pleads Geneva. "It's only one call for you two, but Holland and I are going to be grounded for longer than Lent. We just barely got here, and it took us so much *work*. Besides, we're safe, right? Because you're looking after us now. Right?"

Ryan scarcely can hold in a smile at Geneva's plea. "Let's wait until after breakfast," he advises. "Conversations flow better on a full stomach." Dana seems unsure. She has to think a moment before she agrees with a short nod. The mood turns more cheerful as breakfast takes shape. Ryan cracks eggs into foamy omelettes while I pulp bananas for the muffins. Geneva makes coffee and pours juice. When we sit, I am reminded of our coffee afternoons with Annie.

"I wish you could have met our friend," I mention. "I don't think she's coming back."

"No," agrees Geneva, tight-lipped. "She's gone."

"Did she have family . . . other people to visit?" Dana asks.

"She had to make sure we got here safely," Geneva says. "Her job's done now. She's gone." I notice Dana and Ryan exchange a covert glance of skepticism.

"Can we go to the beach today?" I ask.

"I'm a fantastic swimmer," Geneva adds. "If you want to see."

"We'll pack a picnic," Dana suggests. "Spend the day at the ocean. There's so much to see, too much to fit inside a weekend. You girls need to come again. . . . A full vacation, in the fall—"

"After hurricane season," Ryan interrupts. "December's best, especially for birding, after the migratory—"

"Not that young girls would be interested in birding," Dana cuts in. "But there are some amazing species; driving up, we saw a clay-colored robin and a bare-eyed thrush, both visible without our binoculars."

Ryan and Dana Hubbard remind me more of their matching-binoculars photograph once they start talking about their hobbies, and it's easy to see how well they get along. They keep interrupting each other as they discuss their bird-watching and nature hikes and favorite Seattle restaurants. In turn, they pepper us with questions about school and the parents. The morning is long and talky, full of second and third helpings and refilled cups of coffee. When I push away from the table, my stomach pooches the skin of my bathing suit, but I feel wonderfully full.

Ryan washes the dishes while Dana makes a new mess preparing a basket lunch.

"Thanks for breakfast," Geneva says. "I was hungrier than I thought."

"The legendary Shepard appetite," Ryan

says. I catch my reflection in the pan he is toweling dry; I look surprised.

"Did you see them a lot? Before, I mean?" I venture.

"Twice a year, sometimes more," Dana answers. "We would visit your family in Saint Germaine over the kids' winter break, and then they'd all come out to our place in the Catskills in the summer. This was a long while back, before we moved to Seattle. Ryan and I used to stock up an absolute mountain of groceries before they arrived." When she looks over at Ryan, her eyes are sad, but she manages a smile. "I'll go give Lydia a ring," she says.

I decide I had better take matters into my own hands and face the parents' anger before the Hubbards speak with them. I dart out to the front room and reinsert the phone jack, then sit on the couch, take a deep breath, and, after a few bumbles with the zeroes and ones of the long-distance code, call home.

"Hello?"

"Hi, Dad, it's Holland."

"Holland." I hear Mom in the background, the flurry of muffled words between the parents.

"How are you both?"

"How are *we*? How are *you*? We've been

calling nonstop. What were the two of you thinking?"

"Did you get hold of your parents?" Dana calls from behind the kitchen door. "Don't hang up until I have a chance to talk."

"Holland, are you all right?" Mom has the phone now. "This was a very, very stupid thing to do. We haven't slept a wink. We didn't know whether to call the police or the British embassy."

"I have a right," I say, my words stubborn, harsher for the deep distance that separates us.

"Your father and I look so foolish." Mom's whisper sizzles against my ear. "What I don't understand is why you didn't think you could just come to us first. All this secrecy, and no one to look after you. So irresponsible, all of this, it's hard to believe I raised you not to know better. Now listen, your dad says if we phone the embassy, they'll send someone—"

"No, wait, because guess what? Ryan and Dana are here. Isn't that great? We met them and everything. So we do have people taking care of us, okay, Mom?"

There is more agitated mumbling between the parents, but by now both Hubbards are at my side, reaching for the phone. "I'll put Dana on, okay?"

"We—" But before Dad can finish, I pass the receiver to Dana.

"Hello, my dears," she says. "I've just fed your wonderful daughters."

I withdraw to the kitchen.

"How much trouble?" murmurs Geneva.

"Hard to say," I answer.

"Cross your fingers."

The conversation is not long, and mostly I hear Dana saying, "I see," and "Of course," which seems like a good sign. When they come back into the kitchen, the Hubbards' faces are passably serious but not angry.

"I'm not going to lecture, because it's not my duty, and because you'll get plenty of it when you get home," Ryan says as Dana nods in agreement. "Your spontaneity put a few more gray hairs in your parents' heads, but in terms of the weekend, we've got it all smoothed out. I better have a look at your return tickets, though, so we can make arrangements for when your parents need to get you at the airport."

Geneva smiles at her lap, where she's hiding her crossed fingers.

"Strange to hear Lydia's voice. . . ." Dana says, more to herself than to anyone else, as she busies herself with the basket lunch. "Not so changed, but then . . ." There is a wistful twist in her mouth as she remembers. "We went to City College together, you know. Just seventeen when we met."

For Dana's benefit, I make my mouth into an oval of amazement, but it's impossible for me to picture Mom as a young person. She has been old forever, although it is not hard to refocus Dana into an oversized, gangly girl with a swing of black hair and a laugh kind of like Kathlyn's.

Dana holds her nostalgia close throughout the day. I hear her whispering the parents' names to Ryan as we walk ahead of them down the crushed shell trail to the beach, where we set up a big striped umbrella and spread out towels in the sand. But even if the Hubbards are weighted by memories, they pay us so much attention that for the first time in her swimming history, Geneva doesn't have to shout, "Look at me! Look at me!" while she does her water acrobatics.

"You'd think the Queen of England and the Queen of France decided to come visit. I never saw two people get so worked up about meeting a couple of strangers," Geneva says, all smug, after she has worn herself out with headstands and flips.

Ryan has brought along a foam-rubber ball, and the three of us dive into the water for a catching game while Dana suns herself, like Cleopatra on the banks of the Nile. We play Jaws and Monkey in the Middle and a made-up game of catching the ball with left hands only.

The water of Saint Germaine is different from my dreams. It is warm, slivered by cooler currents, and bright enough to see down to my toes. There are fish, too, tiny white schools of fish that look like columns of starlight shooting through sky water.

"This is the best ocean I ever saw," Geneva says. "It's more real than any other water I've ever seen."

"Bluer," I say. "Wetter."

Geneva and I stay in the water long after Ryan gets tired and leaves us, until our underwater skin is soaked pale and our exposed shoulders burn tender with sun, and then we join the Hubbards for lunch. I did not think I could be hungry again after my breakfast feast, but I'm starving. We get a choice of tuna or egg salad sandwiches and apple or grape juice, and we crunch through tangy mouthfuls of potato chips. There is fruit for dessert; the sand that blows into my bitten peach adds a nice grainy seasoning.

"You ought to stay out of the sun for the rest of the day," Dana admonishes my sister as we pack up to leave. "You're turning pink. I remember how Kevin burned easily. Your mother used to make him wear long-sleeved shirts in the middle of the day; otherwise he'd blister. Your skin reminds me of his."

"You think we look alike?" Geneva asks. "Holland and me?"

Dana holds her mouth, thinking. "No," she finally answers. "You both look mostly like yourselves, although you have Kevin's coloring and Holland has something in her that makes me see Elizabeth—I'm not sure what. But the two of you, no. Two very different-looking girls. Now let's hurry and pack up, or we'll be caught in a downpour."

When we get back to the bungalow and are in the bathroom, changing out of our suits into dry clothes, I see how the Saint Germaine sun has separated me from my sister in more ways than how it colors our skin. The salt water has lightened Geneva's hair while the humidity has caused mine to frizzle, and all my freckles stand out, littering my neck and nose, while Geneva's pinkness is smooth, like a boiled Madame Alexander doll.

"Listen." I incline my head. "They're in the kitchen. They're cooking. Again."

"Have you noticed how they both do snorts in their laughs?" Geneva imitates the sound, and we press our hands over our mouths to hold in the giggle attack.

"They're nice," I whisper when I can breathe through the laugh-wriggles that stick in my throat.

"They are," Geneva agrees. "But also they're so . . . *floppy*. The way they talk and eat so much, and laugh with snorts. No wonder the parents stopped liking them. They have nothing in common."

"Nothing in common anymore," I say. "Who knows how it was before."

"They act like how I wish the parents would." Geneva loses her smile as she blurts our thoughts out loud, and her face blushes beneath her sunburn. "They're real people. Being here is awful in a way, because it makes me see how it used to be, before everything, before us."

"How it will be," I reassure her. "We'll come back, Geneva. I promise."

The front room has turned dim and cool. Just as Dana had predicted, an afternoon rain starts, pinging the roof like a popcorn parade, then turning more tidal, washing water over the lawn.

The Hubbards have made tea and warmed up a black-walnut–apple cake. We decide to eat in the front room, lounging in the recliners. The Hubbards sit together on the couch, not truly touching, not Ick, but close enough that Dana's dress laps over Ryan's leg, close enough that they must sense each other's pulse, smell each other's smells. Their togetherness reminds me of the parents; it is one thing they do have in common.

"Why does it rain so hard here?" Geneva asks. Ryan perks up.

"It's because of the tropical hydraulic cycle," he answers. He goes on to explain the rain, describing the weather as the world's most ancient music. Through his words, acts of evaporation, condensation, and precipitation become the movements of a majestic water symphony. After he is finished, we applaud along with the pocking on the roof.

"You sure know a lot about storms," Geneva says.

"Ryan's a meteorologist," Dana explains. "Of course, you girls must get science lessons every other minute with Quentin in the house." I think of Dad, the stripe of light beneath the closed door to his study.

"Are you a scientist, too?" I ask her.

"Obstetrician," she says. "I help deliver babies. I assisted with John, in fact, my first year out of medical school. Didn't your parents ever tell you that?"

"They don't say much about either of you, actually. Not to us, anyway. They're awfully private." A silence follows, and I hope I have not hurt the Hubbards' feelings.

"They turned to each other," Dana remarks after a moment. "It's understandable. That kind of tragedy is hardest on parents. But Ryan and I missed those children, too. Miss them still. We spent some of our happiest times with your family. I suppose it's partly why we keep coming back here." She looks around the room. "Only I had no idea how dusty my memories were until I saw you girls. You shine up everything for me."

I must have napped, lulled by the rain. When I wake up in the front room, the sun has emerged, another juice-bright sunset to match yesterday's. Geneva's chatter calls me to the kitchen. I stumble through the pantry door and see Dana at the counter, busy with her cooking. Geneva and Ryan are on their way outside.

"Aha, look who decided to join us," Ryan says. "You've been sleeping a couple of hours now."

"We're going to look at frogs," Geneva says. "Ryan says they get big as oysters!"

"Big as hamsters," he corrects. "We'll be out back. You coming, Holland?"

"She'll be out in a minute," Dana answers for me. "I need a little help right now."

Once they have banged through the kitchen door, I sit at the table, watching as Dana finishes chopping scallions, which she scrapes from the cutting board into a saucepan of sizzling butter. I get a feeling that Dana wants to tell me something but doesn't know how to begin. The bite of hot scallion juice fills the kitchen and smarts my eyes as I wait.

"Your mother told me everything," she says at last. "All about your imaginary friend, Annie. I had an imaginary friend once, when I was a little girl. I fell off a ladder and broke my leg in three places, and I had to lie flat on my back in a cast for six weeks. I named him Dickins, after the boy in *The Secret Garden*. He came to visit me every day. We'd chat and tell jokes and make plans for all the things we would do together after my leg healed. It saved me, I think. Having a special friend."

"Imaginary?" I laugh. "Annie's not imaginary, she's as real as you or me. She's a painter, she painted that tree in the pantry, and she painted our whole kitchen back home. Why would the parents say such a funny thing? Imaginary, ha."

Dana looks down, examining the flickering blue flame of the stove. "Does that look medium high?" she murmurs to herself. She bites her lip, then adds a hissing shot of water to the pan. "They said you girls got carried away," she remarks. Her voice is matter-of-fact, without judgment. "They said you and Geneva always have been so close, that you almost can hear each other's thoughts, dream each other's dreams."

"Funny, that's exactly how I would describe Mom and Dad."

Dana turns to me and hands me a paper bag. "Break the ends off these beans and put them in here," she says, sliding a colander over the table to rest in front of me. "Anyway, I told Lydia it was for the best that you girls were here, no matter how it came about. Saint Germaine's a place of happy memories. Life ended for those children here, but they were alive here, too. And that's what I remember. Beach picnics and bonfires. The games and laughing. Evenings of gin rummy or watching the stars."

"I wish I'd known them," I say. "I wish I'd been here for those times."

"All your life, people must have told you

about those times," Dana says. "But those days, the other children, they're gone, and the days that matter most lie ahead, not behind you. As for your Annie, she couldn't possibly have created that tree, because I was here, in this very kitchen, the afternoon the boys and Elizabeth painted it. It was a rainy day like this one, and they used an oil paint set of Ryan's. More than twenty years ago, it must have been."

I don't know what to say to this. I stare at Dana, who points to the back door. "The frogs are a sight," she says. "Go on, I'll finish up here."

For dinner we eat fresh parrot fish and string beans, with kiwi tarts for dessert. We spend most of the dinner trying to explain to Geneva why she cannot take a frog back with her to New York. My sister, who disdains all creatures soft and cuddly, has warmed up to the cold-blooded, warty frogs of this island. This is no surprise to me and delights the Hubbards, who can talk as much about frogs as they can discuss birds or stratocumulus clouds or how much sugar is needed to make a kiwi tart.

"Let's go for a walk," Geneva says to me after we have eaten dinner and cleaned up the kitchen. "Just us. To the beach. Please."

"Do you mind?" I ask the Hubbards.

"Take flashlights," says Ryan.

"And sweaters," adds Dana. High cupboards are opened, and giant police flashlights are handed out. Dana rubs our hands and legs with a sticky lotion of mosquito repellent, then buttons each of us into one of her own oversized cotton sweaters.

"Stay close and don't be too long," she calls from the door, "or we'll worry. Don't walk too close to the surf, and for heaven's sake don't go swimming."

They watch us from the patio. For a couple without children, their parenting skills are awfully polished.

We wind down the shell path to the ocean and turn off our flashlights as we sit against the dune embankment. Darkness links its elements: sky and sea meet on a tar-paper crease, sucking sea gushes over its inky beach, black holes of sand swallow our tunneled toes. I keep a thumb on the flashlight switch; it connects me to the promise that the chain of darkness can be broken on my whim.

"Here's the thing, and don't be mad," Geneva says. Out of the corner of my eye, I watch her hands knotting and unclenching in her lap, and I brace myself for her confession.

"Okay. Maybe you figured it out already, but I bought us those tickets. Charged them on Dad's credit card. When the envelope came I sneaked out the receipt and stuffed it in my pocket before you could see."

"You're kidding, right? You mean Dad bought . . . ? Oh, great, Geneva. We are in so much trouble." I flop back on my elbows and groan. "Do you even know how much trouble we're in?"

"Look, I'm sorry. But I wouldn't have done it if it hadn't been for our kitchen and my fortune from Miss Pia."

"What do you mean?" I stare out at the horizon and try to think clearly. So it wasn't Annie after all. I had tried hard to believe the tickets were her gift. Dad will probably want us to pay him back, and two plane tickets are way more than whatever is left of my savings.

"See, the whole time I was painting the kitchen I kept thinking, This is how Saint Germaine looks," Geneva explains. "This is the sky, these are the trees and birds. But as soon as I put in the colors I knew it wouldn't be enough. You can't sit in your kitchen and pretend you're here. It was like Annie painted a postcard on our wall. She knew we'd have to see it for real, once it was up in our kitchen.

And when I got that fortune, about going on a trip, and then you said how people have to make their own fortunes—well, it all just seemed to spin together. I had to get us those tickets, Holland. I had to."

"You know the parents think Annie's imaginary," I say. "They think we made her up."

Geneva pushes her toes deeper in the sand. "It doesn't matter what they think. She didn't come for them," she says. "I'll miss her. She really helped us."

"She isn't coming back."

"No."

"And now I have to be the big sister again," I say half-jokingly. "It was a relaxing break."

"Holland, would you do me a favor?"

"What's that?"

"Will you sometimes call me Neeve? I like it better than my other name, and if you start, maybe it'll catch on with the parents."

The parents would never call my sister by a nickname, an Ick name, and I know this, although I don't say it. There are other, deeper reasons for naming your children after distant lands.

Out loud I say, "Yeah, that sounds better,

Neeve." I am not surprised that the word, once spoken, fits her nicely.

And I don't expect it, but neither does she, perhaps, because Geneva collapses against me as if an unexpected jolt has charged her jittery limbs. Her hug is fierce and hard and alive, over in a crushing second, and with me forever.

twelve

elizabeth

I sleep late the next morning and wake with the sun frying my cheeks. Geneva greets me at the kitchen table wearing a coronet of wildflowers and tells me about sighting a calico monkey that she named Trudy. She and Ryan keep interrupting each other as they describe Trudy sitting on her branch, gorging on bananas. It hasn't taken my sister long to start talking like a Hubbard.

"We practically just got here," I say to Ryan and Dana as we sit down to a breakfast of waffles and cantaloupe. "And now we're leaving."

"But we'll be back soon," Geneva promises. "Holland and I are asking for plane tickets for Christmas."

The Hubbards smile and squeeze us, but I can tell by their petering conversations and by the way they hardly touch their own breakfasts that they are unhappy to see us go. They accompany us to the main island on a speedy boat captained by an old man named Simon whose skin is the color of plums. The morning is fresh, my skin is bright with color and my ears and fingernails are gritty with sand. It feels good, like souvenirs of my trip packed on my body.

Once on shore, we exchange Simon's boat for a cab driven by a woman and her daughter who are on their way back from church. Geneva sits up front with the girl, and they fan each other with the palm leaves brought back from the church service. I sit in back, on one side of Dana, and my mind takes photographs of everything—the rainbow of air, Dana's laugh, the perfume in the sugar cane—a roll of pictures to flip through in my mind until we come back in December.

The airport appears less deserted than when we arrived two days ago. All around us, families are unloading themselves and their belongings from cabs and shuttles.

"The way life worked out, Dana and I weren't able to have children ourselves. Your brothers and sister sure felt like ours, though," Ryan tells Geneva and me as we stand at the gate, waiting to board. He speaks with a half-smile and a casual squint in his eye, but his words draw out careful as a poem. "When they left us, we couldn't have been more devastated than if they'd been our very own. This weekend, seeing you girls, it's all been something of a gift. An unexpected blessing."

He looks as though he might say more, but then he changes the subject, pointing to the sky, and he tells us about how we will likely get some of yesterday's rain when we fly into the city. The language of loss is hard to speak, but thankfully there is always plenty to say about the weather.

"We'll come back soon," I promise as I hug them good-bye.

As I take a last look at the island, I know I have been fooling myself, thinking that I needed to come to Saint Germaine so that Geneva and I would feel closer to our brothers and sister. I had not been truly expecting to find those other people here, not in spirit, not in any way. The real reason I came here was to stake my own claim on this off-limits Eden. Even while I told myself it was for Geneva, or for Elizabeth, John, and Kevin, all along I was betting myself in a secret voice, a voice I was too scared to listen to but knew enough to obey. I wanted Saint Germaine for me.

The parents wait in the terminal. They stand together, wrapped in pale raincoats, as alike as a pair of candlesticks. Ryan was right, I realize. The rain that whipped through Saint Germaine yesterday now drizzles over New York. We've hit the same storm twice.

The parents' hugs are fleshless, like being caught in the press of folding chairs.

"We love you," they whisper in our ears. I cry babyishly, and so does Geneva. I press my face into their rain-freckled coats to wipe my eyes.

When we get home, Mom draws a bath for each of us: mine in the parents' bathroom and Geneva's in ours. After we change into sweatpants and shirts, Mom combs our wet hair and rubs it through with some of her special peppermint leave-in conditioner.

"We should make a beauty salon appointment together, next Saturday," she says. "The three of us. And then have a ladies' lunch after." Her fingers rake through my hair, slicking the peppermint oil from root to tip.

The intimacy of her touch makes me shiver. Never have I felt more like her daughter.

Afterward, we sit in the kitchen. Dad prepares Irish oatmeal, which we eat with spoonfuls of cream and honey.

"I'll be spending more time in this kitchen," he says with forced cheer, "now that you girls have made it look so special."

"As a family, it's important for us to share home activities," Mom says carefully. I can almost see Dr. Bushnell, like the Wizard of Oz behind the kitchen door, prompting her words.

When I get the courage to face our mural, I now see how the paintings are amateurish, that our colors are impulsive, and that nothing fits together. Geneva is talented, but she is still a sixth grader; the plumes of her bird's head look like a bulky headdress of eggplants. My sky is splotchy in places where I remember getting bored. Louis's tree takes up an entire wall. And where is Annie's work? In the long olive grass, in the rain-heavy sky? I cannot find her. I do not know exactly what I had been looking at before.

The parents don't feel comfortable talking about Annie, not that night, nor any time after. Their mouths are dry with bookish phrases fed to them by Dr. Bushnell, about how they wanted to encourage our self-expression, how we created Annie as an escapist manifestation of our subconscious will, how the mural was a means of asserting our need to make our own mark on this house, to paint over the shadow of the other Shepards. Assertion, expression, creativity—they are thoughtful words, the well-intentioned words of grown-ups. Paint therapy, really; I was right all along.

"Then you never really believed in Annie?"

Dad frowns; he opens his mouth to speak and then stops as another, milder expression shapes his face, and he folds my hands between the two of his. "When you and your sister began working on your painting," he begins, "you can imagine that at first these stories of Annie were troubling—*perplexing*—to your mother and me."

"Then why didn't you just say so?"

He is quiet a moment. "We did say so, to Dr. Bushnell, who explained to your mother and me about imaginary friends. Like Nini or Nono, remember? The little girl who lived under the dining room table and ate Geneva's vegetables?" He smiles. "Every night your mother and I would have to sweep the carrots and Brussels sprouts from under her chair."

"Come on, Dad. That was a long time ago."

"Maybe so, but like before, we held back

because you girls seemed so captured. Captured by changing the walls and making the room into something new. I think of your faces at your mother's birthday dinner, and the way your sister was talking. And we just assumed you must have seen a picture, somehow heard about the tree in Saint Germaine."

"No, that's not true. I never . . ." Even as I protest, I am not so sure. I look at Dad helplessly, embarrassed. When Dad speaks again, his voice and words are careful.

"Ever since you were a little girl, you've been sensitive to the stories and memories of Elizabeth. Always asking us about her, what was she like, what kind of daughter, sister, student was she? When you created this older sister figure, even calling her Annie, just a variation of Ann, Elizabeth's confirmation name, we thought—"

"That I invented Annie? Why would I?"

I see in Dad's face that he has asked himself this same question. "We thought you girls needed Annie. To take her away from you didn't seem right."

The gentleness of his tone, his obvious yearning for peace between us, is mesmerizing. My fingers are warm inside the prayer clasp of his hands, and I decide not to upset him any more with my insistence of the truth. Because who is to say which version of our story is the one to believe?

I discuss Annie with Geneva, but these talks aren't very satisfying. "I wish other people had known her, had seen her," I mention. "There isn't any evidence that she came. Everything we used to paint the kitchen was right here all along."

We have found the paints and brushes, rags and mixers all stacked neatly in the cellar. The art books are in the den, wedged between a giant atlas and a stack of *Life* magazines in a dark corner of the back bookshelf. Their spines pop when we reopen their covers, and their pages are limp with mildew.

"It doesn't matter," Geneva tells me. "Why do you have to find the scientific proof of everything?"

Except that my sister is looking for proof, too, not of Annie but of change. I think Geneva genuinely believed that our trip to Saint Germaine would open the doors to a new and improved Shepard family. For a while, she was as watchful as a gull over our activities, waiting for the crumbs to drop from our rituals. Eventually she began to squawk with conversational bids such as, "We should grill hot dogs on the roof sometime. Hot dogs are my favorite food," or, "Sophie's parents are taking all their kids white-water rafting this summer. I think we should do stuff like that."

"Really, Geneva," Dad would remark mildly. "You seem quite energetic tonight."

Being older, I know better. I know the parents will not take down the portraits of the other Shepards any more than they will roll up the bottoms of their pants and grill hot dogs on our roof. They will continue to meet in the twilight kingdom of their dining room, and their grief is a feast of pain I cannot touch. But now I know that I will not always sit at their table. Life has to keep going.

We end up doing little things to bring Annie back into our home. We leave the kitchen window open all the time, now that the weather is warmer. We have been to MoMA, at first just to look at *Starry Night*, but lately we have ventured off to the photography and film exhibits.

Some days, after school, we brew up a pot of coffee, although we have never been able to duplicate Annie's special blend, and we drink it in our clumsy, ugly, gorgeous birds of paradise kitchen. It has become the center of our home, our favorite place to talk or do homework, and sometimes to open mail from the Hubbards, who are back in Seattle now and often send us packages or postcards. We are probably going to visit Seattle next summer, just Geneva and me. Dr. Bushnell has encouraged it.

"I'm glad we have our kitchen," I say. "It's a safe place, kind of a protection. Like Saint Jude."

"How can Saint Jude be protection?" Geneva scoffs as she carefully erases a line on the pastel she is working on. Not long after our trip, the parents enrolled Geneva in an after-school art program at The New School, and since then she has been preoccupied with her plastic one-snap portfolio, her watercolor sets and brushes, and her criticisms of other students in her class. "He's the saint of hopeless cases."

I flush. "Nuh-uh. Louis told me he's the saint of travel."

"Believe what you want, but we just finished our chapter on saints in religion class, so I should know."

"Well, all I know is he helped us," I say. "You can't take that away from him."

"You don't have to get on the defensive just because Litterbug mixed up his saints," Geneva says. "When I get old enough to like a guy, I'm going to make sure he's a smart one."

214

Saint Jude stays under my pillow, though. When I think about it later, it doesn't seem like such a mix-up, and I can't fault myself for believing in the things that comfort me.

With Geneva in art class, my after-school time is free to watch Louis play softball or to hang out with him at the Chatterbox Diner. Louis and I introduced Kathlyn to Louis's friend Paul Santillo, and after some begging, the parents have allowed me to see Louis officially on weekend double dates with Kathlyn and Paul, as long as I tell them exactly where I'm going and am home by ten. As for my afternoons spent at the Chatterbox or the Bishop Brown sports court, I figure part of my time spent with Louis ought to remain secret.

"Some things are more important than rules," I tell him.

"Whatever you say, Sarge," he answers. "You're the boss." Which is becoming especially true these days. After one polite but firm conversation, Dad backed off the science internship, and Mom never mentions the name Aaron Hill in a context of his being at all datable. It isn't until Brett and Carla come over for dinner later that spring, though, that the parents acknowledge what I have realized for a while.

"The older she gets, the more Holland

reminds me of Elizabeth," Brett says after the table is cleared and Geneva and I are excused. His voice is low, but still audible from where I am, in the kitchen.

"Yes, she has something of Elizabeth's spirit," Mom agrees.

If I do, it was given to me at a time when I needed an older sister most, and holding onto her spirit is as close as I can come to safeguarding real memories of the sister I used to have. But it's enough for me.

If I want other stories, I go to Pia, who loves to talk about her high school days. Plus, she reads my fortune, a different one each time, and if I don't bring Geneva, she includes lots of good, Ick details about my love life. Pia also tells me about Elizabeth's boyfriend.

"Such a doll," she remembers. "William Jacowski, but we all called him Jack. Four grades under me, but even us seniors thought he was cute. And now he's an actor, I heard, mostly in television commercials. Actually, I thought I saw him in a heartburn ad. Might not have been him, though. I'm not good with faces."

I can't help occasionally tempting myself, clicking through channels, hoping to see his commercial, and one afternoon after school I search out his pictures in Kevin's senior year

Bishop Brown yearbook. There he is, a smear of dark and light in the third row on the basketball team, there again in a crowded cafeteria shot, and again on page seventy-two, my favorite, above the caption WILLIAM JACOWSKI ADDS A TOUCH OF CLASS TO BBHS'S NINTH GRADE VALENTINE'S DAY SEMIFORMAL. He wears a painted tuxedo T-shirt and holds out his plastic champagne glass in a toast to the photographer. I know Elizabeth is next to him; although she stands just outside the frame, I can almost see her standing beside him in her tap shoes and chenille-covered tutu.

I replace the yearbook in its place with all the others in the den, then I walk into the kitchen, where I retrieve a small paring knife from one of the drawers.

"You got a phone call on call waiting, but I was on with Sophie," Geneva says. She is seated at the banquette, sketching a still life from a bowl of grapes and apples arranged in front of her. "It was Litterbug. He said to call back."

"Okay."

"And I set the table without you."

"Thanks, Neeve."

"Do you like my apples?"

"Your grapes are better." I plant a big noisy kiss on her cheek.

"Yuck," she says.

I walk up the stairs to the Korean chest room, where I sit at Elizabeth's desk and trace over the letters E. S. + W. J. with my fingernail. I slide the knife from my pocket and carve my own set of initials, H. S. + L. L., next to hers. My cut is fresher, but the two hearts could be twins, beating together inside the piney wood. I swipe the lacy crumbles of blue-painted wood chips to the floor and slip the knife back in my pocket. The fading sun filters through the curtains, and for the first time I think the cream-of-tomato rug and asparagus wallpaper do not look so bad. Maybe I will have a sleep-over here sometime. It might be kind of fun.

Faintly, very faintly, I think I catch a scent through the room of vanilla nutmeg coffee.

Then I get up to call Louis.

	DATE DUE		
NOV 2 3 200?			
Sept 2			
	WITHDRAWN		